ESCAPE TO EXILE

STONECROFT SAGA 1

B.N. RUNDELL

WOLFPACK PUBLISHING
— EST 2013 —

WOLFPACK PUBLISHING

—— EST 2013 ——

Escape To Exile

Paperback Edition
Copyright © 2020 B.N. Rundell

Wolfpack Publishing
6032 Wheat Penny Avenue
Las Vegas, NV 89122

wolfpackpublishing.com

This book is a work of fiction. Any references to historical events, real
people or real places are used fictitiously. Other names, characters,
places and events are products of the author's imagination, and any
resemblance to actual events, places or persons, living or dead, is
entirely coincidental.

Paperback ISBN 978-1-64119-852-3
eBook ISBN 978-1-64119-851-6

ESCAPE TO EXILE

DEDICATION

The beginning of a new series can tax the patience of a saint! And yet my first-line editor, my faithful wife of fifty three plus years, has lovingly and patiently put up with my many efforts of bouncing new ideas and characters around in our conversations. But most importantly, when I get that faraway look in my eyes and have deaf ears for anything of the present, she simply smiles and goes on with her tasks of lovingly taking care of this old man. So, once again, I dedicate this work to her and her illimitable patience and love, without which it would never happen.

And to the many readers that have asked about this series, here 'tis! I hope you enjoy it, and if you do, leave a review. If you don't, shhhh, don't tell anybody, but you can drop me a message, and I'll try harder to please you next time! Thanks to each and every one who makes it possible for me to do this, my publisher, Mike Bray, and his wonderful staff, most importantly, Rachel Del Grosso, and the many readers and friends. Thank you!

1 / Duel

The tall hemlocks and white pines in the park-like setting on the south bank of the Delaware River moved but little in the cool morning breeze. The twittering song of the bobolink was cut short by the call of a goshawk with its continual *kaw* that sounded the alarm of danger. A brief moment of stillness was shattered by the barking of two Wogdon and Barton dueling pistols that sounded like angry cur dogs and spat fire and smoke. The two men stood twenty paces apart, clouds of grey-white smoke briefly obscuring each. They had turned to face one another, pistols cocked, and triggers set, their fingers lightly touching the hair triggers. At the shouted command, they turned to face one another, with the older man taking a quick but careless aim and touching off his shot first which was quickly answered by the tall younger man.

Gabriel Stonecroft slapped at his left upper arm as blood blossomed through the silken shirt sleeve. The ruffles at the wrist of the hand that held the pistol caught some of the crimson that flowed from the wound. He looked across the clearing, seeing the result of his shot, and shook his head as he dropped his gaze to the pistol still gripped in his right hand.

The other man, Jason Wilson, an experienced duelist, grabbed at his neck where red stained the torn cravat that now appeared tangled at his throat. His knees buckled as he fell forward, unable to catch himself before his face hit the grass and dirt. He lost his grip on his pistol. Two men rushed to his side, both kneeling beside him, one frantically trying to stay the flow of blood as the other shook his head, mumbling to himself. He lifted his eyes to the opponent and watched as two men hustled him away, shielding his back with their own.

"I believe you've killed him!" declared Ezra Blackwell, the lifetime friend of the combatant, Gabriel Stonecroft.

"I didn't want to!" answered the sandy-haired man. Only nineteen, he was just over six feet tall, pushed the scale at 190 pounds, with broad shoulders and tapered hips. He showed the stature and masculinity most admired by women and envied by men. With a square jaw, high cheekbones, hazel-green eyes, and dark eyebrows that accented his piercing gaze and his chiseled features, he would be considered handsome by any standard. For two years, he had been an honor student at the College of Philadelphia, but he was most at home in the woods, where he and his lifetime friend, now his second, Ezra Blackwell, spent most of their time.

"We had an agreement that we wouldn't draw blood, but when his shot took me in the arm, I had to answer in kind!" explained Gabriel.

"You had no choice," added the man on his left. Doctor Crittendon had accompanied many to their duels, and as a long-time friend of the Stonecroft family, he had not hesitated to join Gabriel and Ezra for their bout of honor.

Gabriel had acted in defense of his sister's honor when Jason Wilson had made some lewd suggestions to her at a party that was considered a prominent social event in Philadelphia in the presence of her friends and her brother. When Gabriel stepped forward to demand an apology, Jason Wilson laughed, both at Gabriel and his sister, Gweneth.

"Hah! Neither of you is worth an apology, even if one was called for!" shouted the impudent man, slurring his words as he tried to steady himself on a nearby handrail. Wilson was from a prominent and wealthy family, his father serving on the Second Continental Congress and his mother's brother, John Rutledge, one of the first justices of the Supreme Court. Jason Wilson was a ne'er-do-well who had the reputation of a drunkard, but his family had always tolerated his behavior, and their influence had kept him out of jail.

Gabriel stepped forward but was stopped by his sister's hand on his arm. His nostrils flared as he turned to Jason Wilson, "My second will call on you to set the time and place for our meeting!" he snarled, breathing deep as he fought his own restraint.

"So be it!" Wilson laughed, then stumbled from the room. Those nearby were silent and turned away to leave, knowing nothing could be said to avert what each one knew was coming.

The three men stepped into the waiting rowboat, manned by two hired sailors, to return to the north shore of the river and the carriage that would return them to the family estate. Gabriel stared at the back of his friend, Ezra. Although a little shorter than Gabriel, Ezra was a powerfully built man, broad-shouldered and deep-chested. In Gabriel's mind, he was as strong as an ox. Ezra was the oldest son of one of the first pastors of the Mother Bethel African Methodist Episcopal Church, and the two had been inseparable friends from childhood. It was, at the least, unusual for a negro to act as second to a gentleman in a duel, but Gabriel would consider no other. The role of the second was to supervise the loading of the pistols, and the second of the offended party would have the choice of positions, pistols, and would also call the cadence or count the steps as the duelists stepped off to their places before turning to fire. It was also their duty if anyone did not abide by the rules, to enforce them, even to shooting the offender. But this duel had gone strictly by the rules of the *Code Duello*, and the only offense had been the broken word of Wilson after the two had agreed to shed no blood.

Ezra breathed deep and turned on the seat to look at his friend. "You know, this won't be the end of it."

"I'm afraid you're right. As cantankerous as Jason was, his father is worse!" answered Gabriel.

"He was their only son," explained the doctor, "and his father always bailed that boy out of trouble and never made him take any of the consequences. You know, of course, that he's been in three duels before this, and killed them all?"

"Yessir, I knew that. But after what he said and did with Gweneth, I couldn't let it slide. "My father taught me to stand up for myself and my family. I can't count the times he said, 'Son, our family name is the most precious commodity we have. Never, never, never do anything that would bring shame on it, nor allow anyone else to do so!'"

"Did he know about this?" asked Joshua Crittendon.

"No, sir. I wanted to settle things first. I know he wouldn't want me to do it, but neither would he try to talk me out of it. He places a high value on a man's character, as well he should, and as he always taught me to do, but he might have wanted to take my place, and I couldn't have that."

"Unless I miss my guess, Old Man Wilson will either come after you himself, or he'll hire some thugs to do the deed for him. I would think you should disappear, at least for a while, and maybe this will blow over."

"Doc, you know it won't blow over. Even if the old man were to hunt me down and kill me, he wouldn't be satisfied. I think he'll try to destroy everything and everyone," suggested Gabriel.

"You might be right," replied the doctor as he lifted his eyes to the nearing shore. "Do you want me to accompany you home?"

Gabriel looked down at his bandaged arm, "I think this'll be all right. Anything special I need to do?"

"Just change the bandage, keep the wound clean, maybe put a little alcohol on the wound, and that's about it."

"Thanks, Doctor," answered Gabriel, then looking to Ezra, "I'll just have Ezra here tend to it. He's pretty good with that kinda stuff."

Ezra grinned, "I'm gonna take great pleasure pouring alcohol on that wound!"

"I bet you will," chuckled Gabriel, standing to leave the boat.

They took the doctor to his office, then started to the family estate. Gabriel turned to Ezra, "So, what do you think? Will I need to leave the country?"

A slight grin tugged at the corners of his friend's mouth, and Ezra chuckled as he answered, "If I didn't know better, I'd think you'd planned it this way. You've always wanted to strike out for the wilderness and leave all this civilization behind!"

"Wanna come with me?" asked the grinning Gabriel, watching his friend try to keep from smiling.

It was an impressive historic two-story brick home, built by the secretary to William Penn, James Logan, and had six curtained windows that stared down from the second floor as if showing their displeasure with the young man of the house. Three gables framed by two towering chimneys overlooked the estate and a circular roadway that enabled visitors to step from their carriages within mere steps of the front door. When Gabriel and Ezra stepped down, Gabriel lifted his hand toward the driver, "Thanks, Thomas!" and dismissed the coach. The two friends walked into the home and were greeted by the Stonecroft patriarch, Boettcher Hamilton Stonecroft, who was standing at the foot of the stairs, elbow on the newel post at the end of the banister. The man had built his sizable inheritance into a massive fortune with wise investments in shipping and manufacturing, reaping considerable profits by supplying the Continental Army with weapons and cannon. He now looked at his only heir with skepticism, relief, and consternation. His furrowed brow showed his concern as he waved the two into the study.

"Well, I am relieved to see you walking, and apparently not too badly injured. After what your sister told me, I can't say as I blame you. But what about Wilson?" asked the elder statesman.

"I believe him to be dead," explained Gabriel, somber-faced but looking directly at his father.

The older man sighed heavily, "I was afraid of that. I believe you have no other recourse than to leave immediately."

Gabriel had not expected his father to be so adamant and had hoped he might have some alternative. He leaned forward, "What do you suggest?"

"Get as far away as you can, as quick as you can."

"But what about you and Gweneth?"

"Don't concern yourself with us. I believe your sister will soon wed Hamilton Claiborne, and he is bound to take her to Washington."

"Washington? Why there?"

"They're already talking about moving the capitol to Washington and he is soon to have his law license, and I believe they are a good match."

"But won't the senior Wilson come after you if I'm not here?" asked Gabriel, scowling as he scooted to the edge of his chair.

"Hah! That popinjay doesn't have near the influence and

money he pretends to have! Oh, don't get me wrong, he'll try to exact some kind of revenge, but he'll send some thugs, and when they find out you've gone, he won't dare lift a hand against me! I'll have his head in a handbasket! Hah!" he pronounced with a smack of his fist on the desktop. He stood up behind the desk, leaned forward, "Besides, haven't you always wanted to try your hand at exploring the wilderness?"

Gabriel was surprised by his father's suggestion, this man had always emphasized education and position, but he now stood to his feet to turn aside, "Of course, I have. Every time I walked into this room," he waved his arm toward the walls, which were mounted with maps, elk antlers, gunracks, and other weaponry that told of his father's many exploits and adventures, both here and abroad, "from the first time you told me of your hunts with Grandfather and your fighting with Morgan's Sharpshooters, I've wanted to have my own adventures. Not for trophies or battles, but to explore and see more of this great land!"

Mr. Stonecroft glanced at Ezra, "What about you? It seems to me every time he," motioning to his son, "went into the woods, you were with him!"

"I'd sure like to, but I don't know what my father would say," answered Ezra.

"Suppose you go find out and get back if you can!"

Ezra jumped to his feet, waved to his friend, and ran to the door. Boettcher Stonecroft turned to his son, "So, what say we start getting you packed?" suggested his smiling father.

2 / Departure

He doffed his silk blouse for a coarse linen hunting shirt, his breeches and spatterdashes for durable linen trousers, and his cravat gave way to a neckerchief. Buckled shoes were surrendered in favor of boots, and his waistcoat and coat were replaced by a woolen greatcoat. Even the tricorn was replaced by a broadbrimmed felt hat. Gabriel stood before his father, hands held out to his sides to model his new attire, and his father grinned. "If I didn't know it was you, I would find it quite difficult to recognize you."

"As you said, the wardrobe of a gentleman is not suitable for the wilderness. I hope to find an Indian village, perhaps Potawatomi, and trade for some buckskins."

"That would be wise. When I went with your grandfather, we both wore buckskins, but of course, that was many years ago," mused Boettcher. "Come, join me in the study."

As they stepped into the man's lair, Gabriel noticed several items arrayed on the old man's desk. He watched his father pick up the smaller item, a finely crafted Flemish knife, "This is the type of knife used by the Coureur de Bois, and both fit this sheath." He pointed to the leather sheath that held the drop-point knives, one about thirteen inches and the second about eight. "You can carry it at your belt, in your boot, or between your shoulders at your back, or you can add a neck thong." Handing the knives and sheath to his son, he turned back to the desk and picked up a rifle. He grinned as he handed it to Gabriel.

"But Father, that's your Ferguson!"

"That's right, and if you remember, there were only five of us in the Sharpshooters during the War of Independence who were equipped with them. But you know all that, and you've proven you know how to use this. Don't forget, use beeswax on the breech screw every, oh, fifty rounds or so."

"I am honored that you would allow me to take it, Father."

The grey-haired man dropped his eyes, cleared his throat as he turned, "And this, you've wanted it since you first used it!" When he turned back to face his son, he held a Mongol recurved composite bow in his hands. Although unstrung, Gabriel recognized it as his weapon of choice. He had become expert with the powerful weapon, using it many times during his forays into the woods. With a core of bamboo, horn on the belly, and sinew on the back, it was all bound together with animal glue and covered with a thin layer of birch-bark. With an effective range of five hundred yards in the hands of a master, it had often proved more lethal than a common rifle or musket. Boettcher held it and the hard leather quiver full of arrows that measured over a yard long, with the tailfeathers of an eagle for fletching. "Now, there are three whistling arrows in there, but the others have metal blades for points."

"Father, this is the pride of your collection!" declared an astounded Gabriel.

"Yes, but that didn't stop you from sneaking it out every chance you got!" answered the elder, chuckling. "Now, I suggest you take your pick of the other rifles to have as a back-up, and probably one for Ezra, if he's coming. Now, here," he picked up an obviously heavy draw-string pouch, "is enough gold to keep you well-supplied for some time. You should also purchase some trade goods to be used as you travel. However, I will make arrangements with my lawyer, Sutterfield, to set up an account at the bank for you to draw on as needed. The details are written out and in the pouch." He paused and leaned back to sit on the edge of the desk, then lifted his eyes to his son. "I'm getting old, and I don't know how much time I have left," he held up his hand to stay the objections of his son, "I have made out my will, and except for a pittance of an allowance for Gwyneth, my estate will be liquidated and deposited in the account that will be set up by Sutterfield. It will be at your disposal, and probably your heirs' as well."

Gabriel took the Ferguson, the Mongol bow in its sheath, the quiver, and the pouch of gold, while Boettcher carried the knives, spare rifle, and the possibles pouch and powder horn. They had just stepped out the back door and started toward the livery when they were hailed by Ezra, riding his cross-bred, long-legged bay horse. "Hey! Looks like I'll be taggin' along! That is, if the invitation is still open?"

Gabriel chuckled, "Of course it is, and honestly, I don't think I'd know what to do in the woods if you weren't by my side!"

"Well, somebody's gotta protect you since you're so prone to getting into trouble at every turn!" he announced as he stepped down.

As they walked into the livery, the cook and house manager, Daniel, was bent over two large leather panniers, stuffing them full of supplies for the journey. Boettcher turned to his son, "I asked Daniel to load up the packs with ample goods and hardware, and the sorrel will do for your packhorse. She's nice and steady and won't spook at much of anything, so you won't need to concern yourself about your packhorse running off with all your equipment." He walked to the first stall and stopped, then put his armload down beside the stall door, and turned to smile at his son.

"You don't mean . . ." started Gabriel, but was stopped by his father's upheld hand.

"Yes, I do. Ebony here is the best traveling horse I have, and you will definitely need him. Besides, ever since I bought him from that gypsy," nodding at the stall, "he's been chompin' at the bit to get out where he can stretch his legs."

Gabriel stepped to the half-door and reached up to stroke the head and cheeks of the black horse, who answered with a low rumble and using his lips to nibble at Gabriel's arm. The two had been friends and companions for over a year since he first came to the family and had been together on all the recent journeys into the woods. Standing just shy of sixteen hands, long-backed, with a big rump and well-muscled forequarters, the stallion lacked a touch of color anywhere, so the name "Ebony" suited him well.

"According to that gypsy, this horse is of the Andalusian breed, and that long mane and tail are typical of show horses, but where you're going, you might want to trim 'em up a mite," suggested Boettcher. "Also, since you'll be traveling incognito, I suggest you take my saddle instead of that fancy one of yours. With a fancy horse and saddle under you, you won't pass for a typical farmer or laborer. So, trim him up first chance you get."

His father's saddle was similar to the Dragoon saddles, with two holsters for pistols, beside the minimal pommel, metal stirrups, and thongs for a bedroll behind the cantle. As he lifted the saddle, he saw that the holsters both contained pistols, but he hastily finished saddling the horse, led him out of the stall and into the light. He was closely followed by Daniel leading the sorrel packhorse, pack and panniers aboard. Gabriel tied on his bedroll, slipped the Ferguson into the scabbard, hung the quiver of arrows beneath the end of his bedroll, and slipped the sheathed bow between the stirrup leather and the fenders.

As he turned, his father said, "I've tied the spare rifles aboard the packs, and there's more powder, lead, and molds in the pannier." He looked wistfully at his son, tears welling up, and held out his arms for an embrace. As the two men hugged one another, nothing was said, but everything was deeply felt. When they stepped back, each forcing a smile, Gabriel was the first to speak, "I will miss you, Father."

"And I you, my son. But even if the duel had not happened, this time was coming upon us anyway. All I can say is, make me proud."

"You know I'll always do my best!" choked Gabriel, quickly turning to mount up.

As he swung his leg over his bedroll, he settled into the seat, then took one last look at his home and his father, "Give Gwyneth a hug for me, and tell her I'll always be thinking of her."

"I will," answered his father simply, stepping back.

The two men rode from the estate into the dwindling light of the day, knowing darkness would soon be upon them, but they were traveling familiar roads, and wanted miles behind them. They rode silently for several miles, until Ezra asked, "You have any idea where we're going?"

Gabriel chuckled, "Into the sunset."

Ezra laughed, "Can't you ever answer a question outright instead of with all that flowery imaginative stuff?"

"How 'bout I just say, into the darkness?"

"Won't be the first time we went somewhere we had no idea where we were or where we were going," grumbled Ezra.

"Well, Ezra, my friend, north is cold, south is hot, and west is unknown. Given the choice, I choose west. How 'bout you?"

"Sounds reasonable. 'Sides, from all we've read about the French, the Spaniards, and others out there, they sound just about as ornery as everybody around here, so . . . don't seem like we got much to lose, 'cepin' our hair to some of those unknown Indians!"

"You're certainly optimistic. How 'bout remembering all those times we used to sit in the woods sharing our dreams of being some great explorers and discovering new territories and finding treasure and all that?"

"'Cuz we ain't kids anymore, in case you hadn't noticed!"

"Ah, but adventure awaits!" declared Gabriel, lifting his arms and laughing as if the entire world belonged to the two of them.

3 / Discovery

When the first light of day began to paint their backs with dimpled shadows, Gabriel and Ezra reined up on the bank of the west branch of Brandywine Creek. The thick oak and hickory woods on the west bank invited them to make camp, and they pushed across the stream as the rising sun bent its first rays into the forest. A small clearing bordered by sparse buttonbush and dogwood offered cover, and the grass invited the horses to graze. They stripped the gear from the horses, and Ezra readied the utensils and foodstuffs as Gabriel fetched some firewood and started a fire. He had become skilled with his flint and steel and quickly had the tinder burning. Soon the fire was ready for Ezra to display his cooking skills.

After putting the coffee on, Gabriel leaned back against the remaining pannier, and as he watched Ezra putzing around, he said, "We made good time last night, and I think I'd like to travel at night again, at least until we get to the Susquehanna. If we push on through the night on the Strasburg road, shouldn't be too many travelers, and we might make it to the river, or at least close to it."

"There was a man in my father's church who had traveled the Susquehanna, huntin' an' such, he said there's a crossing at the road from Strasburg. The river's 'bout three, maybe four feet deep, and the current ain't bad. It's just upstream from a pair of islands and just off the bank."

"Well, dependin' on when we get there, and if the horses' aren't too tired, should be daylight, and we can find us a place to sleep on the other side."

"And after that, we might think about giving the horses a rest 'fore we take to the mountains," advised Ezra as he flipped the meat in the pan. He sat the skillet at the edge of the fire and sat back to let the meat finish cooking, picked up a cup and poured himself some coffee. He glanced across the fire at his friend. "You know, we might not ever come back this way again. Might not ever see any of our family again. You think about that?"

"Constantly. And Ezra, I want you to know a couple things. First, I'm mighty grateful you chose to join me, and second, if and when you ever get to thinking about home and you want to go back, just say the word."

"That's easy for you to say now, but you might not be welcome back there. No tellin' what Ol' Man Wilson will conspire to do. For all we know, he already has somebody on our trail," declared Ezra, sipping his coffee and looking over the brim of the cup, wide-eyed.

"But what I meant was, if you get the hankering to go

home, and even if I can't, don't feel obligated to hold my hand like a schoolkid. You just git and skedaddle! Understand?" responded Gabriel.

Ezra chuckled, "Some folks have said you and me are like two sides of the same coin, course I never asked 'em which one was heads and which was tails, but I ain't about to let you do all the explorin' and adventurin' without me!"

Gabriel grinned, finished his coffee, "Ain't that meat about done?"

"Umm hmm. Get your plate and let's eat!" declared Ezra, pushing himself up to reach for the pan.

The sun was bouncing its golden rays off the surface of the Susquehanna, casting a rippling light on the far bank and the trees and shrubs that lined the edge. A break in the brush marked a seldom-used trail originally traveled by the Lenape, Shawnee, or tribes of the Iroquois Confederacy. Gabriel reached down to stroke the neck of his horse, "Whaddaya think, Ebony? Wanna give it a try?"

Ezra said, "Well, I ain't Ebony, but I think they'll do all right. We kinda took it easy on 'em and the road's been all right, so I say we cross over and fix us sumpin' to eat!"

Gabriel put his heels to Ebony's sides and started into the water. The big black willingly stepped off the slippery bank and walked into the ripples. The gravelly bottom showed shallow and the two small tree-covered islands were no more than thirty yards to their right, but once past the gravel shore, the water deepened and the leather tapaderos barely touched water. The current was slow and the crossing easy, and within moments all three horses were starting to shake as both Gabriel and Ezra stepped down. The rattle of gear and slap of leather made both men step back until the horses finished their shaking, then they led the animals to an opening in the brush and trees that showed a previously used campsite. Once stripped of gear, the horses enjoyed the rubdown given by the men with hands full of grass. Picketed and free to graze, they readily made a meal of the deep green grass.

It was Gabriel's turn to cook and the two switched duties quickly, readying a meal of fried pork belly, fresh duck eggs, and bread dough, rolled out like a long worm and wrapped on a green stick to roast over the fire. Ezra hadn't seen it made before, and scowled a little as he watched his friend angle the green willow sticks over the fire. "Just what do you call that?" asked Ezra, nodding to the sticks.

"Stick-bread, what else?"

"That's bread?"

"Just wait till you bite into it!" declared a confident Gabriel, grinning at the skeptic.

Their campsite offered good cover, yet gave them a clear view of the river, and they agreed it would be a good place to rest up for a spell. They would start their daylight travels on the morrow. Not wanting any of Wilson's hirelings coming upon them without warning, they agreed to spell one another throughout the night to keep watch. Although nothing had happened to make them think they were followed, both preferred caution over carelessness.

Gabriel led the way on the dim trail that wound through the thick woods. It showed no sign of recent travel and in many places was overgrown, but it kept to the due-west direction he wanted. He looked at the towering tulip, oak, and birch trees, seeing many entangled with ivy vines, some he recognized as wisteria and poison ivy. The undergrowth was thick with spicebush, interspersed with buttonbush and dogwood. The trail saw little direct sunlight, and when it broke into the light, the men reined up and enjoyed the warmth of the sun.

"We're making good time, even though it's not a straight line, but we should find us a town in a day or two, maybe get us a meal and a bed for a night before we restock and get into the mountains," suggested Gabriel.

"You know, I've been thinkin' that same thing. That'll give the horses a good rest, and us as well," agreed Ezra.

Gabriel chuckled, "Now, you know you liked that stick bread, so why are you so anxious for a meal from a tavern?"

"I've been thinkin' 'bout how good some tender pork would taste, with potatoes, carrots, onions, you know, all those things we don't have," grinned Ezra.

It wasn't until mid-afternoon of the second day that they broke out of the trees. They had just crossed Codorus creek when they came to a road that showed considerable sign of travel. As they looked up and down on the north-south road, a few cabins showed to the north, and they chose to see what lay in that direction. Shortly, they came to a carved sign that said, Hanover, 2 miles. They looked at one another, grinned, and with nothing more than a nod, started north to Hanover.

They were surprised at the size of the town. Many log homes lined most streets, with several lying in the area beyond and nearer the woods. The main thoroughfare held several hotels, stores, and a variety of other businesses built of brick and limestone. Gabriel spotted a sign swinging from a metal rod that said Sign of the Horse, with a galloping steed as the background. He looked at the broad multi-paned window that had the name painted across the top, with smaller letters that said, This Inn owned by Gerard Reinecker. He glanced at Ezra to see a smiling and nodding face, and after craning around to spot a livery, they pointed the horses to the large stables and were soon walking the boardwalk back to the Inn.

As they pushed through the door, several faces seated at a long bar turned to the newcomers, then, without a word, turned back to their drinks. Gabriel pointed to a corner table, and they seated themselves as a barrel-shaped man with a stained apron stretched across his girth came to stand beside them. He nodded, smiling, and asked, "And how may I help you?"

"First, we'd like a meal and perhaps a tankard of ale, then a room if you have any available," stated Gabriel as he leaned forward on the table.

The innkeeper smiled and nodded again, "Yessir, be 'appy to serve you. We have roast pork with all the fixins' if that suits?" He saw their accepting nods and continued, "I'll be right back with the ale." He turned on his heel and quickly departed to turn their order in to the kitchen, and as he rounded the bar, a large man grabbed at his arm, grumbling something Gabriel could not hear. When the man turned to look in his direction with a scowl on his face, he expected trouble and whispered to Ezra, "Here it comes!"

4 / Clash

They watched the big man stand from his stool, push at the sleeves of his linsey-woolsey shirt, and turn with a scowl toward the two men seated at the table in the corner. The sunlight streamed through the fly-specked window and drew a square of light on the table, showing the rough-hewn boards of the tabletop. Gabriel glanced at Ezra and the gaze was quickly returned as both men looked toward the big man as he stomped their direction. Most of those standing at the long bar turned as he walked behind them, each expecting some kind of commotion. It was a familiar scene to the residents of Hanover, one oft repeated by the bully of the block.

One of the men at the bar spoke, "Martin, why don't you leave 'em alone? They ain't botherin' nobody!"

Martin Knudsen turned quickly to growl at the speaker, "Mind your own business!" and spun back to scowl at the two strangers at the table. He plodded to the table, stretched himself tall, folded his arms across his massive chest, and snarled,

"We don't want none o' yore kind around here! Best you be leavin' 'fore I have to tear you apart an' throw you out in pieces!"

Ezra looked up at the man, showing a disconcerted expression with a wrinkled forehead and wide eyes, "By my kind, do you mean to say you throw all Irish out?"

"Huh?!" asked the man, leaning slightly forward as if he hadn't heard correctly.

"Irish, you know, those of us who have an Irish heritage?"

The scowl returned, "You ain't Irish, you're colored!" he declared, confusion showing as he squinted his eyes and frowned.

"Oh, but most certainly, I am. Me mother's name is Colleen Dubh O'Neil, and we are Celtic descendants of the Black Irish and our heritage goes back to the early Spaniards and the Vikings!"

"Ain't never heard o' no Celtics or whatever you call 'em. You ain't nuthin' but a smart-mouth Negra, an' I'm gonna teach you some manners, boy!" He leaned forward, placing one hand on the edge of the table, and reached for Ezra, who leaned back slightly, just out of reach. Gabriel gave a quick leg-sweep and knocked the legs out from under the bully, making him drop face-first to the table, catching the edge with his chin, stunning him as he fell to the floor. As he scrambled to gain his feet, Gabriel and Ezra both stood, waiting.

Knudsen growled as he lunged toward Ezra and was met with a short jab that splattered his nose, showering his face with blood and stopping his charge. Rocked back on his heels, his wide eyes flared, then he dropped into a slight squat, arms outspread, "I'm gonna break your back!" he threatened as he growled and plodded toward Ezra, more wary after the hit to his face. For a big man, he was surprisingly quick and nimble, and grabbed Ezra in a bear hug, leaning back and squeezing with all his strength.

But Blackwell was as solid as a brick, and as he was lifted off the floor, he leaned his head back and smashed his forehead forward into the man's broken nose, making him cry out in pain and anger and release his grip. As Ezra was dropped to his feet, he sent a quick right jab to the man's jaw, rocking him back, then stepped in with repeated punches to his belly. The bully bent over, surprised by Ezra's strength, and was met with a powerful uppercut that came from the floor, knocking him back and to the floor.

Gabriel stepped to the side of the attacker, leaned over, and as the man shook his head, trying to clear his mind, he said, "You might want to reconsider what you're doin'. My friend has done worse to bigger men than you."

He rolled over, came to his feet, and turned to be met by a roundhouse right that cracked his jaw, obviously breaking the bone and rattling his teeth. He spat out blood, put a hand to his face, then growled again, anger burning in his eyes, and charged. He feinted with his left and caught Ezra with a right cross.

The blow sent stars through Ezra's mind and he staggered to his left, tripped on a chair leg, and went to the floor. The bully roared again, straddled the fallen man, and began punching him in the ribs and beside his head. As he cocked his right for a blow, Gabriel grabbed his arm and spun him off Ezra, sending him to the floor on his back. He looked up and snarled, "So, you want some o' this too, eh?" As he scrambled to his feet, Gabriel said, "I just didn't think it gentlemanly of you to beat on my friend while you held him down, that's all."

"Ain't never pretended to be no gentleman!" he growled as he charged toward Gabriel. The grin of the tall blonde man gave him a quick second thought, but the rolling block that took him over the man's hip and smashed him to the floor caught his attention. He struggled to get his wind and looked up to see the two men leaning over him. The blonde man was saying, "You might want to think about it. Best thing you could do is just shake our hands and go back to your drink. We'll even buy you another one, how 'bout that?"

He got to his feet, caught the thrown bar rag with his face, and glared at the barkeep. Then he looked at the two men, growled, and turned away to return to his drink. Gabriel called out, "Give those men another drink, barkeep!"

The mumbles that came from the group at the bar were friendly, and laughter replaced the complaints and derogatory remarks. Everyone drank up, with many lifting their mugs toward the two in an expression of gratitude. The innkeeper brought plates heaped with the offering of the house, and the large tankards of ale were refilled. He leaned over the table as he filled the tankards and spoke softly, "You might want to be careful about Knudsen. He's not one to let things lie. If he can't have his will one way, he'll try another, and he's not particular how he does it. There have been more than a few travelers who crossed him and were found in a ditch somewhere."

"Why doesn't the town do something about him? Have you no law?" asked Gabriel.

"Hah! Him who calls himself the law spends more time in the tavern than in his office. He's as afraid of Martin as anyone."

"Well, after we eat, we'll turn in for the night, and leave early of the morn. We don't spend too much time worryin' over what might happen," responded Gabriel.

"You can't say you hain't been warned!" replied the innkeeper.

His mother and her mother before her had been known as Banduri, or female Druids. Ezra had many times sat at his mother's feet as she sought to pass on much of her knowledge. She was known to have second sight, and at times Ezra believed he shared that ability. His grandmother had studied for the required nineteen years to learn all the ways of knowledge and healing and had passed that knowledge on to his mother. Although her life was in the new land, her wisdom had been a great help to his father in his ministry, for the ancient druids had also been the spiritual leaders of their people. Her skills in alchemy, medicine, law, and sciences far exceeded the norm, and she eagerly passed as much of that knowledge on to her son as was possible in the time they were together.

Their stop at the local emporium outfitted them with an ample resupply of coffee, sugar, salt, some dried meat, and a few of the early vegetables. The sun was at their backs as they took the road out of town, choosing the north-bound route that would be easy-going and offer a bridge to cross Conewago Creek, ultimately taking them to Gettysburg and a road through the South Mountains via Nichols Gap, or so said the storekeeper at the emporium.

The road had a slight rise and the tall hickory and oak trees lined it, shading the lane. The men rode side by side and the sun shone brightly ahead as Gabriel expressed, "That looks like the road leads straight to heaven," nodding to the crest of the rise which gave the appearance the road did indeed lead straight into the blue.

Suddenly Ezra reined up, frowning, as he looked ahead. "Uh, let me take the lead, then do as I do."

Gabriel had seen that look on his friend's face before, and he knew better than to question him. Several times, that innate ability of his companion had kept them from trouble, and he willingly yielded to his judgment. Nearing the crest, Ezra suddenly dug his heels into the bay horse's ribs, and the animal responded by lunging into a full gallop. Gabriel grabbed one of the horse pistols holstered by his pommel and kicked his black into a run as he brought the pistol to a full cock, setting the trigger. A musket roared, and the bullet whistled just over the head of Ezra, who lay low on his horse's neck. The smoke showed the shooter's location, and the big man dropped his weapon's butt to the ground as he frantically reloaded. But the roar of the pistol in Gabriel's hand of lifted the man's head, open-mouthed as he swallowed the bullet that ripped out the back of his neck, dropping him into the brush at his feet.

Gabriel and Ezra reined up, Gabriel dropped the double-barreled pistol into the holster and quickly drew the second one, bringing it to full cock as he turned back to approach the would-be assailant. He knew his shot had scored, but he didn't know how bad the man was hit and wasn't about to take any chances. Both men dropped to the ground, ground-tied the horses, and carefully pushed through the brush toward the shooter. Within a few steps, they came to the still form of Martin Knudsen, sprawled on his back, sightless eyes staring at the lone cloud in the blue sky.

With the body of the town bully draped over the pack saddle, the two men rode back into Hanover and tied their mounts at the hitchrail in front of the town constable's office. A portly man with galluses showing under his too-small waistcoat, a linen shirt open at the neck, and trousers that showed all of his scuffed high-topped boots, stepped from the office with his thumbs in his trousers and asked, "And what do we have here?"

"This man," started Gabriel as he pulled the body off the pack, letting it drop to the ground in a heap, "tried to waylay us on the road. He missed, I didn't!"

The constable stepped closer, and bent over just enough to recognize Martin Knudsen. He straightened up and looked at Gabriel, "And how do I know that's what happened?"

"Because I said so, and my friend here will attest to that."

"Well, to be perfectly honest with you, I'm not surprised. This man," he motioned to the corpse, "has been thought to have done that very thing before, but no one ever lived long enough to file a complaint. So, good riddance, I say!" He turned back to his office, leaving the two friends staring at his back.

Gabriel looked at Ezra, shrugged, and the two mounted again and resumed their journey. Once out of town, Ezra said, "That was different."

"Wasn't it, though? Maybe that's what the innkeeper meant when he spoke about 'the law' in their town. But I'm not about to complain. I was expecting some kind of investigation or hearing or something, but . . ." he let the thought hang in the air between them, then concluded, "And I'm certain we'll have enough troubles along the way to make us appreciate this."

Ezra chuckled as he glanced at his friend, "Umm hmmm, you usually find some kind of trouble to get us into." Both men laughed as they looked down the long, empty road, trusting in a power greater than theirs to see them through.

4 / Mountains

Leaving Hanover, they determined to fight shy of people and towns, but took to the Gettysburg road until after the bridge over the south branch of Conewago Creek. Taking to the trees, they paralleled the road and stayed out of sight of any travelers. There was an occasional wagon, freighter, or farmer's wagon, as well as other mounted travelers, but none that showed any concern. Once in sight of the South Mountain range, they swung south of Gettysburg to once again take the road that led to Nichols Gap. They passed a couple of nubbin hills as they neared the South Mountain range, but it was the end of the day. They chose a dim trail that led them south of the road into thick woods where they found a campsite with evidence of considerable use. On the west bank of a wide, shallow creek, ample grass offered both graze for the horses and comfortable sleeping for the men.

"There's some wood already here by this old fire ring, but we'll need more," called Ezra as he unpacked the utensils and foodstuffs for their supper.

Gabriel was picketing the horses and answered, "I'll fetch some, but then I'm climbing that mountain behind us. I wanna get a look at our backtrail. It's not often we find a place where we can see further than the next hedgerow or thicket, so I'm gonna have myself a look around."

With his brass telescope in hand, Gabriel climbed the steep brush covered slope of the mountain, which rose almost six hundred feet higher than their camp. Taking a zig-zag course through the brush, using game trails when possible, Gabriel soon topped out on the knob of the mountain. He stood and gazed at the marvelous view of the wide green valley, dotted with nubbin hills, streams, and the occasional plat of a farm or farms. The road that scarred the flats and cut through Nichols Gap stretched back through the woods and plains as far as the diminishing dusk would allow him to see. About a mile and a half east of his mountain and astraddle the road, three buildings appeared to be a traveler's stop.

He put the scope to his eye, stretched it out to focus, and looked at the two-story stone building. It was obviously a stage tavern since he saw a mail stage drawn up at the corral at the side of the building. He watched as four riders came to the corral and dismounted and stripped their horses, turning them into the corral and the lean-to shed. Only one of the horses was distinguishable from the others in that it was a dapple grey, while the others were the more common dark bay or blood sorrel, with nothing of note about them.

The men, one sizable, two common, and one short and

waddling, walked into the tavern, pushing their way past the waiting stage passengers. From a distance, none were recognizable. Gabriel didn't know what he was looking for but made note of the men anyway. Although he fully expected Old Man Wilson to seek some kind of retribution for the loss of his son, he knew there were any number of ways the man might react. But something continually nagged at Gabriel's conscience, and he leaned toward the possibility that the old man would send some hirelings after him and Ezra. He wasn't afraid, knowing he could take care of himself and Ezra could as well, but preparedness was the proper course for them to take.

Just this past summer, Gabriel had traveled with his father to England for his father to attend to some business matters regarding his shipping investments. While there, Boettcher Stonecroft had made arrangements through his associates for Gabriel to have some private instruction from Daniel Mendoza, the three-time champion boxer. Although Mendoza was a rather small man at five feet seven inches and one hundred sixty pounds, he was the only middleweight to win the Heavyweight Champion of the World title. His boxing academy taught his entirely new style of boxing, which focused on "side-stepping" and avoiding blows by ducking and moving around, something that had not been done before where the practice was to stand still and swap punches. After Mendoza, he also had a couple of sessions with the new champion, Gentleman John Jackson. The last month of their stay in England also gave Gabriel the opportunity for instruction in the Akiyama Yōshin-ryū style of Jūjutsu that had recently been introduced to Europe from Japan.

But Gabriel never thought of himself as a fighting man, but the skills learned had bolstered his confidence, of which he had no lack before. Always carrying himself with a straight posture and head high, his friendly smile was disarming and sincere and told little of his skills with his hands and with weapons. Usually soft-spoken, he had never been one to back down, but held to his beliefs and manners, as a man of genuine character.

He made a full scan of the countryside, then stepped closer to the bluff overlooking the road they would take on the morrow. He looked it over, then started off the mountain. As he pushed through the buttonbush, he was startled when a white-tailed deer jumped across the path and scampered away, flag in the air. He chuckled to himself, realizing he had been thinking about home and wondering about his sister and father, hoping they would be immune to any retribution taken by Old Man Wilson. He retraced his steps, noticing fresh bear tracks over his from his ascension to the crest. He bent down and examined the tracks, noting a larger set and two sets of smaller tracks following. "Must be a momma and her cubs," he whispered, looking down the trail and hoping not to see the three. He continued on, seeing where the trio of bears moved off the trail and into the brush, then quickened his pace and was soon at the edge of their camp. "Smells good! Is that some of that pork you got from the innkeeper?"

"It is! It took all I could do to talk him out of it, but we have a fine feast tonight!" answered Ezra, sitting on a flat stone, holding a steaming cup of coffee. Gabriel poured himself a cup and asked, "Is it ready, or do we need to wait?"

Ezra nodded at the tins, "There's your plate, have at it!"

As Gabriel dished up his share, Ezra asked, "See anything?"

"Nothin' special, but there were four horsemen that stopped at the stage tavern back down the road a ways. Oh yeah, and I saw fresh tracks of a bear and her cubs," answered Gabriel, reaching for a coffee cup. As he poured his cup full, the whinny of the black brought his head up. The horse stood, head high, ears forward, nostrils flaring and front feet prancing nervously. Gabriel whirled to look behind him, but nothing moved, and he looked back at the stallion, who was still showing nervousness. He turned back to search the trees, and a movement near the top of a tall hickory caught his attention. A black ball of fur was peering from the high fork of the tree, little black eyes focused on the men at the fire. Another one scampered up behind him, and both clung to the rough barked branches. Suddenly a growl came from the foot of the tree behind a thicket of dogwood, and Gabriel knew who the visitors were. He looked at Ezra, "Take it easy, and move to the horses. We need to settle 'em down, and it might be good to have a rifle handy."

They backed away from the fire, each with a tin plate in one hand and a coffee cup in the other as they neared the picketed horses. Gabriel set his utensils down and, speaking softly, he held out a hand to the black, approaching slowly. "Easy boy, easy, it's all right. Easy, now." His back was to the fire and the distant bear, but he saw the flared eyes of Ebony looking past him and undoubtedly watching the black disturbances. He reached out to touch his black just as the momma bear let out another angry growl. Ebony pulled back, but Gabriel latched onto the halter rope and held him tight. Ezra wasn't as close to his big bay, and at the growl, the horse reared up, jerking the peg from the ground and in an instant, he had whirled on his hind feet, dropped to all fours, and disappeared into the trees at a run. Ezra reached for the lead rope of the sorrel packhorse, catching it just in time, and stepped close to reassure the mare.

Both men, holding tight to the lead ropes, turned to look toward the bear. They saw the momma bear had climbed the tree and swatted the lower cub, who started backpedaling down the tree as she reached for the higher of the two. She caught his rump in her teeth, gently pulled to make him release his grip on the limb, and as she started backing down the tree, he was close behind. They soon were out of sight behind the tall brush and undergrowth, and as the men listened, they heard the three padding away into the deeper woods.

With a little more reassurance by speaking and stroking, the black and the sorrel soon settled down and went back to grazing. The men picked up their tins and Ezra said, "Let's finish eating and give that crazy gelding of mine a chance to settle down. Maybe he'll come back on his own. If not, then we can go after him. I don't think he'll be far; he usually settles down pretty quick."

"Well, I'm all for eating. I'm so hungry my belly button's pinching my backbone!" declared Gabriel as he forked the pork and vegetables into his mouth. They had traveled far on this day, not stopping for their usual nooning, but dusk was dropping the curtain of darkness, and the horse had to be found. With a few quick bites and a chug of coffee, the men swung aboard the horses bareback and started after the wandering gelding. Ezra knew his horse; less than a quarter-mile from camp, in the middle of a park like meadow, the big bay had his head deep in the grass, tail swishing at flies, acting like nothing had happened. He was quickly retrieved and led back to camp, where all three were again picketed at the edge of the clearing.

They turned in as the stars began to light their lanterns for the night, and Gabriel lay with hands behind his head, looking to the heavens. He spotted some constellations he recognized, remembering how he and his father often sat on the back courtyard and talked about the stars and the world and the things of God. Although the family had often attended Christ Church, the church anybody who was somebody attended, he had often struggled with his own personal relationship with God. He smiled at the thought of his family seated on the wooden pews in the church. It was the church with the steeple that made it the tallest building in North America, and the arched windows and elegant interior with fluted columns that set it apart from the usual church buildings of the time. Even the baptismal font claimed fame, having been used by the rector, William White, who was now the presiding bishop of the Episcopal church, to baptize William Penn. It wasn't unusual to see many of the signers of the Declaration of Independence in the pews, and even Betsy Ross, who was read out of the Quaker Meeting house because she had married John Ross, an assistant rector of Christ Church.

But the rigid formality with the rector's robes, chanted prayers, and the ringing of bells and all just seemed to leave Gabriel wanting. It wasn't religion he sought, but that personal closeness the Bible spoke about with Jesus and his disciples, and even John the Baptist. He remembered reading in the gospel of John about being "born again," and he wanted to know more. Maybe Ezra could shed some light on things for him. After all, his father was a pastor, so he just might have the answers. Gabriel smiled at the thought, let his eyes rove across the heavens, and soon drifted off to sleep.

6 / Direction

"What is it that has you so deep in thought this fine morning?" asked Ezra, sipping his morning coffee and looking across the remaining coals of the cookfire at Gabriel.

"Huh?" asked Gabriel, coming out of the daze that had him staring with glazed eyes at the smoldering coals. He looked at his friend, eyebrows raised, mouth slightly open, but otherwise expressionless.

"You've been staring at the fire since before we ate, and now that coffee that you usually require to be so hot it would burn the average man is cold. So, you've been somewhere in that overactive mind of yours. Where were you?".

Gabriel brought his eyes into focus as he chuckled at his friend and poured his coffee back into the pot, pushing it to the coals. He looked up at Ezra, "Just thinkin'. We've been doin' more running away from what's back in Philly than going somewhere. I think it's time we decide just where we're going and why." He reached for a long stick to stir the coals, adding a piece of firewood to give heat to the coffee.

"Well, it seems to me the why is pretty obvious. It's the where and maybe the when that's the question. We've always talked about the wilderness, and from what we've studied and know, the wilderness is just about anything west of Pittsburgh. Wouldn't you say?" asked Ezra, leaning forward with his elbows on his knees.

"Yes, or at least, it used to be!" declared Gabriel, then scooting forward and using the stick, began to draw in the dirt. "We're here, and Pittsburgh is here, 'bout five or six days away, right?" He looked at Ezra for agreement.

"Ummhumm, 'bout that, I s'pose," he replied.

"Now, the Ohio river starts there, goes west," he made a looping line to his left, looking at Ezra to ensure the man was following, "and way down here, it comes to the Mississippi. That river," he drew a new line, longer and straighter than the first, "runs basically from the north," he pointed with his stick, "south to New Orleans. And everything to the west is now Spanish territory. As you know, it used to be French, but now it's Spanish."

"All right, so?" asked Ezra.

"I've been keepin' up on things; the Philadelphia Gazette has been pretty good about that lately and this area north of the Ohio is attracting a lot of settlers. Several of those who served in the War of Independence have received Federal Land Warrants, and that land along the Ohio has attracted quite a few of them."

"But it wasn't that long ago that the Northwest Indian

Wars were goin' on there," mentioned Ezra, a scowl painting his face.

"Ahh, that's been over for some time now." He turned back to his drawing in the dirt, "And a lot of this land," pointing to the south of the Ohio, "already has settlements and such. But," he paused to look up at Ezra, grinning, "west of the Mississippi, that's where the real frontier is, and as far as I know, it has very few settlers and just a few towns." He sat back, stick across his lap, smiling.

"So, if I'm hearing you right, you're thinkin' we need to go west of the Mississippi?"

"Yup, that's what I'm thinkin', all right."

"And do what?" asked Ezra.

"Explore! Don't you get it? Look," he pointed to his scrawls again, "settlements here, here, here, and more happening all the time. Eventually, the only place for people to find new land will be west of the Mississippi. And if we're there first, we'll have our pick of anything! And even if we don't want to have land, we'll know all about it and can do as we will, guide others, map it out, anything!" declared Gabriel, more enthusiastic than Ezra had seen him in a long time.

The enthusiasm was contagious, and Ezra began to smile as wide as his friend, then grabbed the coffee pot and poured himself another cup before offering one to Gabriel, "Let's drink to it!"

The excitement of a new direction gave special energy to the two as they broke camp and started through the gap. It was early morning, and the sun stretched long shadows before them. The quiet of the valley was broken only by the clatter of their horses' hooves. Each man had retreated into his own thoughts, and given their active imaginations, their future took on all manner of adventures. Once through the gap, they made good time across the flats, traveling on established roads and passing few travelers.

"I'm surprised we're not seeing more travelers," mused Gabriel.

Ezra looked at his friend, "That's because today is the Lord's day, and most folks are in church or at home instead of traveling like us heathens!" declared Ezra.

"Well, why didn't you say so? We coulda had our own church service, or tried to make it into a town and go to one," suggested Gabriel.

Ezra reined up and looked askance at his friend, "I didn't think you were too interested in the things of God."

Gabriel turned around to gaze at his friend, "That ain't so. I've got plenty of interest, but not a lot of knowledge. Maybe you can teach me a few things on this journey, what say?"

Ezra grinned, "And my pa thought I was takin' to the road to perdition." He raised his voice and sat tall in the saddle, motioning with his outstretched arms, "Little did he know his son was gonna be preachin' the Word all across this big country!"

Gabriel laughed at his friend, "Now, don't go gettin' all fired up about it. I do want to learn, but that doesn't mean you have to preach to me every day!"

Ezra laughed, "I think we both have a lot to learn. But I did notice you have a Bible in your saddle bags, am I right?"

"Yeah, you're right," drawled a reluctant Gabriel, grinning at his friend.

The sun was bright in their faces as it dropped to be cradled by the long ridge of the North Mountains. As they came to the west branch of the Conococheague Creek, a wide shallow creek with thickly forested banks, with the west bank rising about seventy feet above the creek bottom, covered with brush and scraggly trees. As they reined up, Gabriel turned to Ezra, "How's about we do a little huntin' for some fresh meat?"

Ezra grinned, "It's about time we did somethin' useful. I would thoroughly enjoy settin' some fresh venison steaks to sizzlin' over the fire."

Ezra started downstream and Gabriel went upstream. With his Mongol bow in hand, Gabriel thought about the many times he had taken it into the woods for the various excursions the two had taken in their younger years. It was all he could do to draw the bow half the length of the arrows, but even then, it had proven deadly on the turkeys and rabbits he was allowed to hunt. When his father had given him his first flintlock rifle, the bow had been returned to his father's weapons display and had seldom been used afterward. Now that he could bring the bow to full draw, he was anxious to try it on bigger game, hopefully, a white-tail deer.

Just a few moments after leaving the camp, Gabriel heard the report of a rifle from downstream. He was certain it was Ezra and he grinned, thinking his friend had taken the first game. He moved quietly through the trees, picking his way among the undergrowth and the entanglement of fallen branches and more. A sudden flash of movement caught his attention and he froze in place, then moved to the side, trying to see through the dense woods. The flare of white told of a fleeing deer. An unexpected shot sounded, coming from the direction the deer had fled, and Gabriel bent low to try to get a better view.

He heard the rhythmic footfalls of a fleeing animal, but the animal was coming closer. He saw the tan of a deer, lifted his bow, and waited as the denizen of the woods stumbled toward him, obviously wounded, but not mortally. Gabriel watched and waited, and once it stepped into the slight opening between the big hickories, he let fly his arrow. It buried itself just behind the front leg, deep in the low chest of the buck, and the deer took two steps and fell on its chin to lie still.

Gabriel waited, knowing that whoever had taken the shot with the rifle was probably trailing the deer, hopeful of finding it soon. He didn't want to step out and be in a compromising position at what someone else might perceive as their kill. A short while passed as he stood quietly behind the big oak, and then he heard tentative footsteps carefully following the blood trail of the deer. He watched as what appeared to be a young man approached. When the hunter spotted the downed deer, he stood tall, grinned, and walked quickly to the carcass.

Gabriel watched as the young man came near, poked the deer with his rifle, and when there was no movement, he knelt beside the animal. He reached out to touch its side, and Gabriel heard, "Boy, you're a nice one. We're gonna be eatin' good now!" But the voice was not what Gabriel expected. Then he heard, "Wait, what . . .?" Gabriel grinned, knowing the hunter had spotted the arrow. The hunter quickly stood, rifle in hand, and looked all around, probably fearful of seeing some Indian coming after the deer.

"Whoa there, take it easy," said Gabriel as he slowly stepped out from behind the tree. "That's my arrow you see," he said as he slowly walked closer, both hands uplifted.

The young hunter saw the bow in Gabriel's hand and asked, "You shot it?"

"Ummhumm, I did. But you scored the first hit so rightfully, it's yours."

"My pa said if two shoot the same animal, it oughta be shared. So . . ."

Gabriel looked at the hunter, cocking his head to the side, thinking there was something different about this one. He looked at the rifle, held casually but confidently in the hands, then at the threadbare clothes. It was not unusual for someone in the woods to wear their old clothes, but this one had britches that were too big, rolled up at the cuff, and several patches showing. The linsey-woolsey shirt was obviously from someone much larger, and the bare feet didn't appear to have ever worn shoes, but the face was clean, and the floppy felt hat had a lot of hair tucked up into it.

Gabriel asked, "What's your name?"

"Why?" retorted the youngster.

"Mine's Gabriel. Just bein' friendly. You need some help dressin' that deer?"

"I can do it. Done it before."

Gabriel chuckled, "Won't that be kinda heavy for you to lug back home?"

The hunter looked from Gabriel to the deer and back again, "I can make more'n one trip."

"Tell you what. I've got a horse back at our camp. You start dressin' the deer, I'll go get my horse, and we can take it to your home in one trip. How would that be?"

"You don't know where I live!"

"No, but I'm sure you can show me."

"Why'd you do that?"

"Just bein' helpful, is all. So, how 'bout that name?" asked Gabriel.

"It's Bet . . . uh . . . Bethel," mumbled the youngster, turning away.

Gabriel frowned, "You mean Betty, don't you?"

The girl turned quickly back to face Gabriel, "How'd you know?!" she asked, appearing a little frightened, with wide eyes and a firm grip on the rifle.

"Whoa! I don't mean no harm. 'Sides, there's absolutely nothing wrong with being a Betty instead of Bethel. And a girl who can shoot like you? Well, you don't have anything at all to be concerned about."

"But I didn't kill it!" she answered, nodding toward the downed deer.

"Sure, you did. He was on his last leg when he got here. I just shot him so we wouldn't have to chase him any further."

She cocked her head to the side as she looked at him, trying to ascertain if he was being truthful or not, then asked, "How come you shoot a bow? Ain't you got no rifle?"

He chuckled, "Yes, I have a rifle. But I like using this. It's a lot quieter, and no one knows where you are!"

She lifted her chin as an answer, then turned and dropped to her knees beside the carcass. She laid her rifle across the rump of the deer, pulled a knife from a scabbard in her hip pocket, and started on the job of dressing the animal. Gabriel smiled and turned away to go to camp for his horse.

7 / Farm

"There, that's the trail!" declared Betty as she pointed. Sitting behind the cantle of the saddle, holding onto Gabriel, the excited girl directed her benefactor to her home. Although happy about her success in hunting, she was somewhat embarrassed to bring this kind man to her home, such as it was, but it was home. The small dwelling was a partial dugout, sod roof, log walls, mud chimney, and one window beside the door. A woman, dressed in gingham, was hanging a few clothes on the line when she heard their approach and turned, wide-eyed, at the sight of a visitor.

Betty leaned around Gabriel, waved at her mother, and called, "Ma, it's me! I got a deer!" Before Gabriel could rein up, the youngster had slipped to the ground and ran to her mother. Although he couldn't hear all that was said, when Betty turned to point at him, he did hear, "Ma, this is Gabriel! He helped me with the deer. That's why I'm home so early!"

Gabriel touched the brim of his hat, "Evenin', ma'am.

Pleased to meet you." He stepped down and went to the pack-horse to remove the carcass. He turned to the woman, "Where would you like me to hang it?" He had glanced around and saw the ramshackle barn with the attached corral but noticed there were no animals nor any recent sign of any.

"Umm, in the barn, I reckon," came the feeble voice of the woman. She was very thin, sallow faced, and appeared quite frail. She gathered her skirt about her and walked before him to the barn. When she pulled open the door, it was with considerable effort, and the hinges creaked from lack of use.

She stood watching as Gabriel hung the carcass from the singletree that swung from the overhead beam. It had apparently been used before and suited the purpose as he split the hocks of the deer and stretched up to spread the hind legs to hang the animal. The block and tackle made it easy to hoist it off the ground, and he quickly tied off the rope to the nearby post. He looked at the carcass and back at the woman, "That'll make it easy for your husband to skin out," he declared, turning toward the woman.

She dropped her eyes, "Ain't got no husband. He got kilt!"

Gabriel frowned, "I'm sorry, ma'am. Was it recent?"

She turned away, looking out the barn door, "Last fall. He'd done harvested the corn an' such, then wanted to get a start on the plowin'. Hitched up ol' Hector, our mule, was plowin' the cornfield and the plowshare broke off'n the frame, spooked the mule and he run away, draggin' muh husband behind. When we found 'em, the mule's leg was broke an' muh husband was all tangled up in the plow handle an' reins an' such, but he was all tore up, broken bones an' such. Didn't last out the night." She stood staring, remembering, one hand on her hip, the other at her mouth. A sob shook her shoulders as she dropped to her knees, her face in her hands.

Gabriel knelt beside her, put one hand gently on her shoulder. "What are you going to do?"

She looked up at him, "Don't rightly know. Ain't got no money. Bank's got a note on the place. What he harvested went to that, but didn't pay it all." She shook her head, sat back on her heels, searching her apron pocket for a hanky, and wiped her tears. She looked at Gabriel, "Please forgive me, didn't mean to start blubberin' like that."

"That's alright ma'am. I understand." He looked around at the barn and out the door at the dugout. "How many acres do you have here?"

"Just a hunnert n' sixty. The usual. Most of it's good land, but I cain't work it, even if I had a mule."

"Have you tried to sell it?"

"Don't nobody wanna pay good money for it when there's so much out yonder they can get for the takin'. But if'n I could, we could go back home."

"Where's home?" asked Gabriel.

"Virginia. Got folks there, up in the Blue Ridge Mountains," she answered as she leaned forward to get up from the ground. Gabriel stood, offered his hand to help her, and they walked together from the barn. Betty had tethered the horses to the hitchrail and leaned her rifle by the door. She had taken off her hat and made an attempt to fix her hair, and stood smiling by the hitchrail.

"Ain't it a beauty, Ma?" she asked, proud of her accomplishment.

"Yes, dear, it's a nice deer. But now we need to get it skinned and let it hang to cool off and cure a mite."

Betty smiled, "I'll get right on it, Ma. Ya want I should cut us some steaks for supper?"

"No, dear, we'll let it cool overnight, an' then we'll have some," answered the woman, watching the girl start for the barn.

Betty turned, "You leavin' us now, Gabriel?"

"Yes, Betty, I'll be leaving."

"Thanks for helpin' me!" she declared, waving as she turned to trot to the barn.

Gabriel waved at the youngster and stood looking around the place. The dim light of fading dusk was little help, but he turned back to the woman. "Ma'am?" then paused, "Uh, what is your name, anyway?"

She smiled a bashful smile, pushing a wisp of hair behind her ear, "Marilu Hatfield," she answered.

"Mrs. Hatfield, if you don't mind my askin', just how much of a note does the bank have on this place?"

"It were a hunnert dollars, but Joe paid 'em forty from the crop."

"Humm, and you say you have a hundred and sixty acres?"

"Yessir, an' most of it's good bottom land. Banker said the whole place was only worth mebbe a hunnert an' twenty, if'n that. Why you askin'?"

"My friend and I have been looking for some land, we want more than this, but . . . this could be a start." As he looked around, he put his hand to his chin, thinking. "How 'bout this? I could give you sixty dollars and take over your note. That would give us a start, and get you a little money to go back to Virginia and your family."

She looked up at the man, frowning, "You'd do that? Really?"

"Yes, ma'am. But, I won't be around to take care of the paperwork at the bank. But if you'll tend to that, I'll put in another ten dollars for your trouble and leave you my name for the banker. How would that be?"

"Oh, sir, that'd be mighty fine. Yessir. Oh my, that'd be wonderful!" she declared.

Gabriel leaned back against the hitchrail, grinning. When the woman clapped her hands, smiling broadly, he watched her start to the house to get something to write the information down. When she had disappeared into the house, he unbuttoned his shirt just enough to access the small pouch behind his belt and took out seven Liberty Cap ten-dollar gold pieces. He put them in his pocket, tucked in his shirt, and smiled as the woman returned from the house. He used the nearby barrel top for a writing desk and wrote out the terms of the purchase and the amount of cash tendered, signed it, and asked her to sign it as well. She very carefully signed her name, and he handed her the pieces of gold.

"Oh, my! I've never seen this much money all at one time!"

"Well, you be careful with that, and don't let anybody see

more than one coin at a time. Now, take this to the banker and leave it with him. When I return, I'll settle up with him."

He looked at the woman, who stood with tears streaming down her cheeks but with smiling eyes.

She looked at Gabriel, "You are my angel, sir. Yes, indeedy. May I hug you?"

Gabriel smiled, dropped his head, and said, "Certainly."

The rising moon gave enough light for Gabriel to find his way back to camp, and he was warmly greeted by Ezra upon his return. As he stripped and picketed the horses, Ezra said, "This turkey sure is mighty fine tasting, but try as I might, I can't get it to taste like a fresh venison steak!"

Gabriel accepted the offered tin and cup of coffee, grinning at his friend, "Now, I just don't understand that. As good a cook as you are, you should be able to work your magic on this scrawny bird!"

"Scrawny?! That bird ain't scrawny! It's fatter than the deer you didn't get!" he chided. "So, what took you so long to haul a *scrawny* deer back to that young'un's home?"

"Oh, nothing much. Just had to take care of buying a farm, that's all," declared Gabriel, trying to keep from grinning as he lifted the big brown drumstick to his mouth.

"You what?!" exclaimed Ezra, mouth agape and leaning forward to see his friend's expression by the firelight.

"Bought a farm."

"What about our exploring?" asked the flabbergasted Ezra, unbelieving.

"We'll still do that. But it never hurts to own land. It's not much, just a hundred and sixty acres of good bottom land."

"What are you going to do with a farm if we're out west exploring?"

"Nothing. It won't go anywhere, and she'll see to things with the banker, so . . ."

"She?"

"The young'un's mother. Look," he started as he placed the drumstick on his tin and reached for his coffee. "The husband was killed last fall, they were on hard times, broke and lookin' like they were starvin', so . . ."

"You always were a soft touch for a sob story!" declared a grinning Ezra.

8 / Pittsburgh

The next several days of travel seemed repetitious; cross a ridge of mountains followed by a long wide and usually fertile valley, another ridge of mountains, another valley. The end of the third day after the farm saw them at the foot of the wider stretch of thick timbered Laurel Hills. Other mountain ridges had shown taller and more distinct mountains, or at least a long ridge of mountains, but the Laurel Hills spanned almost six miles east to west. As had become their custom, they camped on the east edge of the hills and were soon enjoying fresh venison steaks sliced from the young buck taken by Gabriel with his Mongol bow.

As the steaks sizzled over the flames, Gabriel was busy cutting the remaining meat into long, thin strips that could be easily smoked and kept for their journey. He had gathered some chokecherry and black cherry wood to lay across the coals beneath the green willow frames that held the strips. The smoke slowly rose among the strips to dissipate in the canopy of the forest. Ezra looked at Gabriel's handiwork, "You know, that looks like you know what you're doin'. When did you pick up that handy bit of knowledge?"

Gabriel chuckled as he continued cutting the thin strips, "It's amazing what you can learn when you spend time in the library at college. They have books about all sorts of things, even some journals written by early explorers of this land. Who'd a thought they even knew how to write, much less make a book out of all that?"

Ezra cocked his head to the side, grinning, "It's a good thing you stocked up on all that reading because where we're going, the only library you'll find is God's library of the wilderness! And in that library, I might find a thing or two to teach you!"

"No doubt, my friend, no doubt. Say, are those steaks ready?" asked Gabriel, wiping his hands clean and pausing in his labors as he looked at the cookfire.

"Reckon so, and we've even got some Johnnycake to go with," replied Ezra, turning back to the fire.

After inquiries with a passing traveler, Gabriel and Ezra entered Pittsburgh on Braddock's Field Road, proceeded to Grant Street, and at Third Street and Wood, they stabled their horses. The stable hand was a friendly sort, and Gabriel asked, "Have you known of anyone taking their horses downriver?"

The grey-haired colored man looked at Gabriel, forehead wrinkling, "Why, yessuh, I has. Those whut do, though not many of 'em, put 'em on a flatboat, or some on a keelboat. Is that whut you'se wantin' to do?"

"Considerin' it, yes. If we were of a mind to do that, where would we inquire?"

"Why, the boatyard, suh. It be at First and Short Streets."

Gabriel motioned to the horses, "You take special care of those, especially that black, maybe trim up his tail and mane considerable, and," he handed the man a fifty-cent piece, "I'll have another one of those for you when we leave."

The man smiled and nodded, "Yessuh, yessuh, will do, suh!"

With their bedrolls and saddlebags, the two men started down Wood Street to First Street and turned right, walking on the south side on the boardwalk. Ezra looked to his friend, "Sure doesn't smell very good!" motioning to the gutters that carried sewage toward Hoggs Creek.

"I don't think I could live in a city again! I know it's only been a couple of weeks, but . . ." he let the thought hang between them as they looked at the buildings that hugged the narrow street. There were log homes, brick business buildings, and limestone homes and businesses, all crowded together. The traveler had suggested they stay at Sam Sample's Inn and Tavern, one of the older businesses near the river, and within two short blocks, they found the building. They entered the main room, stopping to let their eyes adjust to the darker interior, then walked to a table near the window that faced Ferry Street and seated themselves, stacking their gear against the wall.

Nearby, seated alone at a table, was an old man, with long, grey whiskers and hair over his collar, smoking a corncob pipe and nursing a mug of ale. He watched the newcomers as they were seated, and when they looked his way, he gave a slight nod and looked down at the newspaper on the table before him. Gabriel noticed the man as he glanced up from his paper, then back to the news again.

The innkeeper, a fastidious man with a stub of charcoal and a pad of paper, came to their side, nervously nodding as he asked, "How may I serve you, men?" He had on a clean apron that covered his chest and midriff, hanging to his knees, but he also had on a jacket that covered the top of the apron. He had combed his thin hair across his bald dome and had small spectacles that rested on the end of his nose, reminding Gabriel of Benjamin Franklin, who sat across the aisle from his family in Christ Church.

Gabriel smiled at the man, trying to put him at ease and asked, "Do you have any rooms?"

"Yessir, we do. Would you want one or two?"

Two rooms, and we might be here a few days while we make our arrangements if that's all right?" inquired Gabriel.

"Certainly, sir, and will you be supping with us as well?"

"At least for tonight. What do you recommend?"

"Today's special is our Irish Stew, everyone seems to like it very much," explained the innkeeper, nodding repeatedly and forcing a smile.

"That would be fine. And would you be the one who could answer a few questions about the area and businesses?"

The innkeeper looked from Gabriel to Ezra, then glanced at the window and at the older man seated nearby. He looked again at the man, "Eb, would you be so kind as to answer these gentlemen's questions while I tend to their meal?"

The old man grinned, "Certainly, Wilson, be glad to." He leaned forward and asked, "What can I help you with?"

Both Ezra and Gabriel turned to face the man and Gabriel began, "Well, we were thinking about traveling down the Ohio, wanted to take our horses and gear, but . . ."

"I thought so!" said the man, standing from his chair, and with a motion of his hand toward their table, started toward the empty seat after Gabriel nodded his approval. As he scooted up to the table, Gabriel asked, "What do you mean, 'you thought so?'"

"You both have the look about you." The man grinned and relit his pipe from the candle at the table. "By the way, my name is Ebenezer Scholfield, and it's pleased I am to make your acquaintance."

Gabriel shook his hand, introducing himself and Ezra, and as the man tucked the newspaper under his chair, Ezra asked, "The look?"

"That faraway, bound-for-adventure, devil-may-care look. I recognize it because I once had it! Now, you want to go to the Mississippi, do you?"

"We didn't say anything about the Mississippi," responded Gabriel, brow furrowing.

The older man grinned, "Been there!" he declared, "And that's just the jumping off place for whatever adventure you're seeking!"

"You've been there?" asked Ezra, leaning closer.

The man nodded and exhaled a bit of smoke from the corner of his mouth as he smiled at the two. "And all the way down to New Orleans, and upriver to that new settlement the Frenchies are callin' St. Louis! Lots more places, too!"

He sat back as the innkeeper brought steaming bowls of Irish Stew and tankards of ale for all three. He motioned for the two to start eating, but Ezra bowed his head and Gabriel followed as Ezra softly spoke a prayer of thanksgiving. The old man grinned, "You ain't missionaries, are you?"

Gabriel chuckled, "No, we're not missionaries. However, Ezra here is trying to expand my knowledge concerning the Scriptures."

The old man grinned, "Now, if you're wanting to go down-river, you've come at a most opportune time. With the Whis-key Rebellion put down, there are several men I know that want to take a load of whiskey down to New Orleans. What with the new tax an' all, they need to make a better profit, and they think down south is the answer. They're in need of someone to ride along until they get to the Mississippi, Indian country, you know. And, they could use some help to pay for the building of the flatboat. Now, if you gentlemen would be interested, I can be your go-between, and maybe get you to the frontier."

Gabriel looked from Eb to Ezra and back again, smiling, "That sounds like what we need. But tell us about the frontier; what did you see, and where all did you go?"

"Well, my young friend, that would take more time than I have remaining in this life, but I can tell you what I *didn't* see but wish I had, and that's the mountains they're callin' the Rockies. I've talked to a few that have seen 'em, and believe you me, I wish I was your age so I could give it another go!"

"I've read about them! The French and Spanish have argued about that land for many years, and I've heard that Thomas Jefferson has designs on that country as well, and if he ever becomes President . . ."

"They say those mountains are so high it's like they stand as pillars of the sky!" said Ebenezer, wistfully looking at the window as if he could see them in the distance.

"Now, that's what I'd like to see," declared Ezra, watching the old man with glazed eyes and daydreaming of faraway lands.

Gabriel brought them both back to the present, "But first, we've got to get down the Ohio. So, Mr. Scholfield, can we meet with these men on the morrow?"

"Certainly, certainly!"

"Good, then perhaps you can recommend an emporium for us to re-supply and prepare for this trip?"

He leaned forward and began to tell the two adventurers about two emporiums that would have all the goods they needed and more. "And I will meet you here with my friends, say, mid-afternoon?"

"That would suit us just fine, and thank you, sir," stated Gabriel, smiling hopefully.

9 / Preparations

Gabriel was pleasantly surprised when the clerk at the Western Emporium in Pittsburgh told him they had a Delaware woman who made buckskins and moccasins. "Her husband was a son of ol' Chief Buckongahelas 'fore he was killed at a fight with the Kentucky Militia. Her an' her daughter used to trade here with us, and after that, they came in with a few hides, wantin' to trade and talked 'bout how those hides'd make good buckskins. So, muh boss said, 'Show me!' an' she did. Came back two days later with a fine set. Let's see, that were two year ago, and they been here ever' since. 'Course, there ain't as much call for buckskins as they used to be, back when they was more hunters and trappers goin' up to the Great Lakes country. Would you believe, we used to be busier'n a bunch o' beavers in here all the time, till them Shawnee, Wyandot, and all the others got together to make war on all us'ns."

"But you say they still make buckskins?" asked Gabriel, hopefully.

"Ummhumm, shore do," answered the clerk, adjusting some goods on the shelf behind him.

"All we've got is three hides, ain't tanned or nuthin', but we need two sets o' buckskins each. Can she do that?" interjected Ezra.

"We got a whole shed o' hides, pelts, tanned skins, an' all. The market ain't been so good lately, so, yeah, I reckon her an' her girl can get some put together for ya." He looked at the two men, turned away to summon a young lad who was sweeping the floors, "Junior!" he hollered. As the boy came near, he said, "Go fetch that squaw," nodding his head to the back, "and tell her we got some work for her!"

Gabriel and Ezra looked at one another, grinning. They were happy they would get the buckskins they needed before they left on the river. They had a considerable pile of goods on the counter, and quickly finished their buying and were ready to settle up with the clerk. In the pile were tarpaulins, lead bars, bullet molds, blankets, sugar, cornmeal, flour, and other staples. And although coffee was being imported from Saint-Domingue and was expensive, both Gabriel and Ezra had become accustomed to regular consumption of the brew and made certain they had a good supply.

Gabriel, always the cautious one, had divided the gold coins given to him by his father into several stashes. He now pulled several coins from his pocket and counted them like a miser, shaking his head as if these were the very last he had, even casting a furtive look at Ezra, implying they might not have enough. But when the tally was made, he slowly set the coins, one at a time, on the counter, to the amazement of the wide-eyed clerk. "Those are some o' them new Liberty Cap gold coins! Ain't seen too many o' them. Boy, howdy, they sure is shiny!" he declared, picking one up to examine it closely. Gabriel finished his count with two silver dollars, three five-cent, and two one-cent coins. The clerk counted the coins, looked up at Gabriel with a smile, "Looks like we kinda emptied yore poke!"

"Pert' near. Might have 'nuff left for a meal or two," acknowledged Gabriel. "But at least we got us an outfit!" he concluded, looking from the clerk to Ezra as they started gathering the goods and bundling them in the tarpaulins. What they couldn't carry, they asked the clerk to set aside for their return. They told him they would call back for their buckskins, and the clerk gladly complied.

They stacked their new supplies in the stable with the rest of their gear and opted for a meal at Sample's Inn while they waited for Ebenezer and his friends. The wait was shorter than expected; they had just finished their meal when the old man entered the door of the tavern, looking around for his new acquaintances. At a wave from Gabriel, he grinned widely and walked to their table.

"Afternoon, gents! Are you ready to meet these fellers?" he asked, looking at both men.

Gabriel looked behind the man, "I don't see anybody."

Ebenezer chuckled, "No, no, they're down at the boatyard. I figgered you'd wanna see what they were buildin' and meet 'em there, if'n that's alright?"

"Sure!" declared Gabriel with a glance at Ezra. Both men

rose from their seats to follow the old man to their meeting.

Just a short walk from the Inn, they came to the boatyard that fronted on Short Street and spanned the block from First Street to the bank of the Monongahela River. The yard was fenced, but one could easily see the many men busy at their craft within the yard. As they walked through the gate, the two men looked the yard over, seeing a new keelboat taking shape on jack stands, with half a dozen shirtless men swinging hammers, stuffing oakum, fitting timbers, and others pouring hot pitch as a sealant. It was hard work and required hard men with skills and commitment, for the crafts they built carried men and valuable cargo. At the edge of the yard, a more cumbersome rig was being worked over by three men, each at a separate task. This was a flat-bottomed craft sometimes called a broadhorn, but usually called a flatboat. With a beam of eighteen feet and a length of sixty to sixty-five feet, it was a bulky framed craft with a cabin that stood about six feet above the keel. It was also flat-topped, but a good-sized post stood at the rear, which would be the pivot post for the long sweep that would steer the craft.

Ebenezer looked at the wide-eyed men, chuckled, "Ol' Man Yoder's lettin' 'em build their boat here so he can give 'em any pointers they might need. He's the best boat builder around, and quite a craftsman, he is." He motioned for them to follow him and they walked past two older keelboats, apparently in the yard for repairs and sitting on blocks until the workers could get to them.

"HO! Lucius!" called Ebenezer as they neared the boat. With the hammering, sawing, and shouting going on, he had to shout just to be heard. A pot-bellied, balding man with red cheeks and nose lifted his head with a scowl that quickly turned to a broad smile. He rose from his knees on the deck and climbed down the ladder that leaned against the sides. Once down, he turned, smiling and holding out his hand as Ebenezer introduced Gabriel and Ezra.

"This here's Lucius Schmidt. Most of the goods that'll be goin' are his. The others there," nodding his head to two other men, both sizeable, "also have goods, and will be sharing everything on the trip." After the three men shook hands and spoke simple greetings, Ebenezer addressed himself to the older man, "Lucius, these are the fellas I told you about. They've got three horses and their goods, and want to go at least as far as the Mississippi. Now, whatever arrangements you make is between you," nodding his head to all three men. "I'm goin' over here and talk to those fellas."

Lucius motioned them to a stack of lumber in the shade of the craft, and they sat down as Lucius explained, "What we need is some help, but not so much with the boat. We can handle that. 'Course if you want to help, that's fine too. But what we need is somebody who can help if we get attacked by Indians or some brigand or freebooter. And, it would be helpful if you could do some hunting for fresh meat too."

"So, since we'll be earning our keep, we won't need to pay?" asked Ezra.

The man smiled, looked at the hanky in his hand, ran it

over his almost bald head to wipe the sweat, and said, "No, you won't have to pay, but it will cost five dollars for each of your horses!" laughing.

Gabriel chuckled, "All right, we'll do it. How soon do we leave?"

Lucius stood and extended his hand to shake and seal the deal, "We load up tomorrow at dusk, all but your horses, of course, then we push off at first light day after tomorrow!"

As they shook hands, Gabriel asked, "You've made this trip before, I assume?"

"*Ja, ja*, two times."

"How long will it take us to reach the Mississippi?" asked Gabriel.

"Oh, two months, give or take," nodded the portly man, "but to go on to New Orleans, *Ja*, another month, maybe."

Gabriel looked at his friend, "Well, Ezra, looks like that'll take care of most of the summer. We'll have to find us some-place to spend the winter 'fore we go too far."

Ezra chuckled, "Listen to you! We ain't even out of Penn-sylvania, and already you've got us spending the winter who-knows-where!"

"It never hurts to plan, my friend," answered Gabriel as they turned to leave the boatyard.

10 / River

The sun lay low on the western horizon above the treetops that lined the Monongahela. Gabriel and Ezra led their three horses, all loaded, the packhorse with her packsaddle and panniers and a bundle atop, the saddle horses with saddles that held the tarpaulin bundles strapped tightly aboard. The men had purchased a goodly supply of trade goods, anticipating trading with the many Indian tribes in the Far West. "You know we'll have to get us another packhorse, don't you?" suggested Ezra as they neared the boatyard.

"Ummhumm, it'll be along shortly," drawled a grinning Gabriel.

"Huh?"

"I made a deal with the stableman. He'll bring it along soon's he gets another packsaddle for us."

Ezra stopped, looking to his friend, "When'd you do that?"

"This mornin' 'fore you got up for breakfast."

"Well, if that don't beat all," exclaimed Ezra, starting again for the boat.

"Yes, and there's more."

"What do you mean, more?" asked Ezra, not liking the tone used by Gabriel, one of seriousness that usually boded no good.

"Remember me telling you about four riders I saw back when we were at Nichols Gap, just 'fore we entered the mountains?"

"Ummhumm, I remember. You said there were four men, but the only identifier was one was a big man ridin' a dapple grey."

"Did you notice the four new horses in the stalls at the stable, one of 'em bein' a dapple grey?"

Ezra stopped again, looking at his friend, "Aw, probably just a coincidence. Ain't like there's a shortage of dapple-grey horses!"

The three men, who Gabriel found out were neighboring farmers, were at the boat. This would be the second trip for Fredric Guernsey, a man who hailed from the bailiwick of Guernsey in the British Isles, and the first trip for Hamish McSwain, a second-generation farmer whose family came from Scotland but claimed Norse heritage. Lucius Schmidt, the leader of the group and the pilot of the boat, was from a German family that had migrated to America when he was but a babe in arms.

The flatboat had been launched and now sat in the water, gently rocking in the passing current. Two wagons were on the shore beside the boat, partially unloaded, and it was obvious the men had already packed the boat with at least one wagon's cargo, if not more. Ezra and Gabriel removed the packs and panniers from the horses, and while Gabriel led the horses to a makeshift corral in the corner of the boatyard, Ezra started carting the goods to the boat. Hamish, the big Scot, directed Ezra to a back corner of the long cabin for them to store their goods.

Gabriel put the horses in the small corral, then brushed them down and gave them a good portion of grain before he left. As he walked to the boat, he noticed Ebenezer standing near the gate to the boatyard talking with another man, both looking in the direction of the flatboat. The stranger was a well-attired man of about thirty with a tricorn hat and a long waistcoat, and even from a distance, Gabriel noticed the man's distorted nose. He was gesticulating as he spoke with Ebenezer, obviously angry about something, and often pointed toward the flatboat. Gabriel thought it odd, but put the image out of his mind and went to help the others.

The rear of the boat had a large pole corral divided in two where the horses would be kept. One side was already loaded with several weaner pigs and a stack of packed chicken coops. Ezra was surprised to see such a menagerie, but allowed that Lucius and company were well prepared for whatever the voyage downriver would offer. As he stacked their gear in the corner, he looked around the interior of the long cabin, noting it was loaded to the ceiling on one side, with the near side soon to be equal. Barrels of whiskey stacked two high lined the front on either side of the door. With a door on the front and another at the back, the windows were shuttered, but the goods were arranged to allow access. He rightly assumed from the shooting slots in the shutters that the aisles were for defense against any number of perils.

As he hopped from the boat to the shore, Ezra glanced at Gabriel and they picked up more goods to load, and Ezra said, "I thought this was a bunch of farmers takin' their goods to New Orleans, but that boat is loaded! There's cookstoves, cast cookware, lead, barrels of whiskey, and lime, as well as the farm goods of flax, honey, beeswax, lard, tobacco, and more."

"Well, from what ol' Ebenezer said, they make stops along the way and trade with settlers and Indians alike."

"So that's what all them pigs an' chickens are for, eh?"

"Ezekiel from the stable brought the other horse, so we're set," stated Gabriel, struggling under the tarpaulin bundle. When they finished loading their gear, they went to the wagons to help the others.

With bags of potatoes on their shoulders, Ezra and Gabriel walked up the planks to the boat and into the cabin to stack the goods. As dusk dropped its cover of darkness, the only light came from a pair of lanterns on the fore corners of the cabin and the reflected glow of the rising moon off the water of the river. The five men gathered at the sandbox stove in the bow of the boat as Lucius poured cups of coffee for each one. He looked around the circle, grinned, and lifted his cup, "To a profitable voyage!"

"Hear, hear!" declared the others as they lifted their cups to one another.

With the eastern skies showing a scalloped skirt of grey, the lines were cast, and the flatboat pushed away from the bank. Ezra and Gabriel had loaded the horses in the gray light of early morning. With Hamish and Fredric manning the sweep oars on each side from their perches atop the cabin and Lucius handling the steering-oar or sweep, the boat was soon in the current and pushing past the waters of the Allegheny and into the combined flow of the Ohio River. With the ramparts and bastions of Fort Pitt fading behind them, smiles were painted on all faces, with everyone anticipating the voyage.

Lucius had instructed Ezra and Gabriel about sawyers and sandbars and had assigned them the job of lookouts. They soon passed Brunot Island and Montour Island as the river pushed on its northerly course. Their excitement kept them busy throughout the day, and they chose to have jerky and apples for their nooning, with occasional cups of tea to pass the time. They made good time, and as dusk settled in, they pushed to the north shore as the Ohio made a sweeping bend back on itself at the confluence with the Beaver River. As the boat nosed into the mud at the bank, Hamish jumped ashore, line over his shoulder to make the boat secure, tying it off fore and aft to big hickory trees, whose overhanging branches offered some shelter.

Fredric had already started his cooking duties at the sand-box stove, a ten-plate Valentine Eckert stove from the Sally Ann Furnace Works in Pennsylvania. It was one of several stoves on board, and would probably not last till the end of the voyage, as most would be traded to early settlers on the way. But atop the stove, Fredric had a skillet with sizzling pork steaks and a pot with potatoes and carrots. In the small oven, biscuits were baking, and the men were promised a good meal for their first night aboard.

"Now, I don't know how much everyone knows, but I thought it best to make sure you were all aware of what we're heading into," began Lucius as the men sat back on the crates after their meal, sipping their coffee. "From here on out, we'll be in what most would say is Indian territory. I've been through this country twice before, but this time, well, it shouldn't be as bad. Since General 'Mad' Anthony Wayne did his deed at the battle of Fallen Timbers last fall, most folks think the Western Confederacy and all the other tribes, are ready to make peace, and the rumor is, they'll be meetin' up with Wayne before winter and signing those peace treaties." He paused, taking a big drink of his own coffee, then started to continue but was interrupted by Hamish.

"What I heard was ol' Turkey Foot got his Ottawas and Ojibwas together with Roundhead and his Wyandots, and they sent word they were ready for peace!"

"Yeah, but that leaves Buckongahelas' Delawares, whose country this has been." He motioned around where they were, "And Blue Jacket's Shawnees haven't shown they're ready yet. And don't forget about the Miamis under Little Turtle. Any of 'em could bring a lot of trouble to river travelers as well as any settlers. And if I know anything about Indians, is that no one really knows anything about Indians. At any time, a bunch of renegades from any of the tribes could strike out on a raid and cause all sorts of commotion. And it would only take one bunch that was that well-armed, and the five of us couldn't hold 'em off."

"If it's that bad, what'd we even start off on this trip?" asked Fredric, shrugging his shoulders and holding out an open palm toward Lucius.

Lucius dropped his eyes and chuckled, "For the profit, Fred; you know that. All of us need the profit from this venture to make it through the winter. Don't know about you, but I've got plans for that money. The wife wants a better home, and I can't blame her. I'm plumb tired of that dugout."

The other two nodded, thinking about their own plans. Lucius looked to at Gabriel, "What about you two? You want to jump ship?"

Gabriel chuckled as he looked at Ezra, then back at Lucius, "Nope. We knew what we'd be facing when we left home. And the only thing we're interested in is thataway," nodding his head to the west.

The renewed commitment seemed to relax everyone, and the conversation turned to more optimistic topics. The five-man crew was getting acquainted and finding common ground to build their friendships upon. It was to be a long journey, and men worked better together when they had mutual interests and commitments. But the future would soon test the mettle of those friendships.

11 / Chase

"Five hunnert dollars is a lot of money, but split four ways, ain't so much!" declared the big, shaggy-haired man, Franklin Kavanagh. He had never been selective with the jobs he accepted, having been a striker in New York City, and this job promised an easy payday. In a time and place where you could hire somebody killed for as little as a couple of ten-dollar gold pieces, a hundred dollars was a lot of money. However, after almost a week of searching and finding nothing, he was questioning the man who hired him for the job.

"Look, Kavanagh," came the raspy voice of the man who was the opposite of the complainer. Where Kavanagh was tall, and as big as a whiskey barrel, the kind of man who bullied his way through life, Shaheen Steinberg, usually called "Shorty" because of his short bow-legs and low-to-the-ground build, he was also the one who arranged the jobs for the men. "Five hundred dollars split four ways is still more'n a hundred dollars apiece, and that's more than you can make in six months!

That is, if you could ever get an honest job. Besides, that five hundred is just for finding him. If we bring him back alive, there's another five hundred, or if we bring his head in a bucket, same thing."

"Well, why didn't you say so?!" exclaimed the big man.

"I did once, but you were probably too busy imbibing to pay attention!"

"Huh? What's that imbi,…imbibe, whatever?"

"He means you was drunk!" growled Hitch. The man sat in a chair, leaning back on the rear legs, and spat tobacco juice at a bucket, missing. His scarred and pock-marked face, added to an angry countenance with slit eyes and a snarling mouth, had others calling him "Badger," but never to his face. The only name he ever admitted to was Hitchcock and usually allowed others to call him "Hitch." Most would say he was a man who would as soon slit your throat as look at you, and most would willingly walk around him. Some would even cross the street to avoid coming anywhere near him. When Kavanagh looked like he was going to respond to the remark, Hitch dropped the chair to all fours, slipped his knife from the scabbard in his boot-top, and showed his tobacco-stained teeth in a lop-sided grin that dared the big man to try something. But Kavanagh, for all his bullying ways, knew better.

The fourth man at the table, Warner Burns, leaned forward, forearms on the edge of the table as he reached for his mug of beer. He took a long draught and wiped his mouth on his sleeve, then sat back. Never one to say much, he stared at the big, dirty window that showed the backward letters spelling Morgan's Pub.

"But we've been on the trail most of a week, an' ever' place we stop, ain't nobody seen no high-class gentleman travelin' with a Negra!" complained Kavanagh. "We prob'ly went the wrong way! I tol' ya they musta went east to the big cities!"

"That's what most would expect, and that's exactly why I'm certain they are going west! According to old Mr. Wilson, he knew Gabriel Stonecroft to be a man of the woods and an adventurer at heart. I'm almost certain we'll find something in Pittsburgh, but if not, then we'll try another way."

"All right, that suits me!" responded Kavanagh, then he looked at the others, "What 'bout you fellas?"

Hitch growled as he nodded, Burns briefly nodded without taking his eyes from the window, and Shorty grinned as he spoke, "Then it's settled." He looked around at the room and bunks, "We'll leave this miserable stage tavern in the morning, first thing. Perhaps we can make Pittsburgh in a week if we don't find them before that time!"

Pittsburgh was a welcome sight for the travelers. Having found nothing that told of the passage of Gabriel Stonecroft and his companion, most of the group was hopeful Pittsburgh would also yield nothing, so they could start back to their usual stomping grounds of Philadelphia. Then they stabled their horses at the livery at the corner of Third and Wood, known simply as "the Stable." Too tired to bother with anything more than a place for a drink and something to eat, they walked from the dark stable into the remaining daylight without a thought about Stonecroft. Although the stable hand looked them over, he said nothing to the rough-looking bunch, having learned a long time ago that most folks would find no fault with silence.

Morrow's Green Tree Tavern was the first open door that enticed the four men, and they soon found a table, a willing barmaid, and an offering of food and drink. After they filled themselves on a rather tasteless stew, Shorty asked the barmaid, "We're looking for some friends of ours, a young man, a good-looking and well-dressed gentleman, with a rather solicitous Negra at his side. Have you seen the sort?"

"Why, no, sir! And believe you me, if'n I'da seen a fine-looking young gentleman, I'da noticed him right off!" answered the buxom wench, laughing with a wide smile that showed her missing teeth. Her scoop-necked blouse showing more than her personality as she poured more whiskey into the men's glasses. Kavanagh grinned as he pulled the woman closer, "You noticed me, din'chu, honey?!"

She laughed, pushing away, "Careful, now. Ya dinna want me to spill the whiskey, now do ya?" she asked as she toddled off to the bar.

"We don't have time for that!" admonished Shorty, "We need to split up and make the rounds of the taverns. If they've been here, someone must have seen them. The sooner we find out, the sooner we can take after 'em or turn back."

Kavanagh and Warner went one way, Hitch and Shorty the other. They had agreed to check each of the taverns and ask questions. Shorty had admonished them, "And watch the drinkin'! Won't do us any good if you're too drunk to remember what you learned. And don't go gettin' into any fights! We don't want anybody to remember us askin' questions, and they won't, as long as you don't give 'em something else to remember!"

"We cain't go askin' questions without buyin' a drink or two!" sniveled Kavanagh.

"It's the two or more that cause problems! So," then looking at Warner, "you keep an eye on him!" pointing to Kavanagh. With only a hint of a head bob, Shorty turned away, and with a motion to Hitch, they parted company with the other pair.

Shorty and Hitch crossed the street to Watson's Tavern, and as they pushed through the door, Shorty looked over his shoulder to see the other two rounding the corner onto Market Street, headed north. The short man and the pock-faced, always angry Hitch found a table, and Hitch growled at the innkeeper, "Bring us a couple mugs!" When the maid arrived, she shied away from Hitch as she set the beer steins on the table. Shorty asked, "Miss, we're lookin' for some friends of our'n. A young man, good sized and well-dressed, traveling with a Negra manservant. Would you happen to have seen them?"

The maid looked at Shorty, "Why, no, sir. Ain't nobody like that been in today."

"Well, it could have been anytime in the last week or so," he asked, eyebrows raised in question.

"Hummm, let me think. Not that I remember. We've 'ad a few gents in, but none with a Negra manservant. But I missed a couple days. I can ask the barkeep if'n ya want."

"Thank you, miss. I would like you to ask him for me if you would."

Again, the answer was no, and the two downed their drinks and left.

Kavanagh led the way for him and Burns as they made their way north on Market Street. He glanced to the side as they crossed Fourth Street and saw a carved wooden sign swinging in the evening breeze. Recognizing enough to know it said Tavern, Kavanagh slapped Burns' arm and motioned with a head nod as he started down the street. They stepped into the dark interior, looked around, saw a corner table with a flickering candle, and wound their way through the other occupied tables to take a seat. Several of the seated patrons grumbled as they passed, but Kavanagh was not one to pay much attention to gripers and complainers unless he was in the mood for a fight. As he thought about it, he was pretty close to being in the mood.

He looked up as a grey-haired colored man in a long, stained clerk's apron asked, "Somethin' to drink, suh?"

"Yeah," snarled Kavanagh. "Two mugs of ale, an' be quick about it!" he demanded. The server paused as if to say something, but turned away and went to the bar for the drinks. When he returned, Kavanagh asked, "Say, we be lookin' for a couple fellers. One is a gentleman-type, fancy-dressed, tall, and he's got him a Negra with him. Seen 'em?"

The server looked at him, and with a slight wave around,

"Suh, if'n a colored man came in here, no one would notice."

Kavanagh looked as the man waved and saw that every one of the patrons at the tables were colored men. Of the eight tables and six stools at the bar, every one had men of color seated, and they all turned to face the two at the table with the server. "Fact is," continued the server, "I don't recall ever having a 'gentleman' like you described in my establishment. Perhaps you didn't notice the sign out front. 'Ben Richards' Black Bear Tavern." He stepped back, hands on his hips, "I'm Ben Richards! And this is my tavern!"

Warner Burns looked at Kavanagh and back at Richards, and after one long draught from his drink, he rose, put a coin on the table, and left without a word. The other patrons stepped aside to allow him to leave. Richards turned to Kavanagh, "Now, if you would like to follow your friend, you may. But if you would like to see how we handle 'gentlemen' in this tavern . . ."

Kavanagh looked at the man, his anger rising and his fighting blood beginning to boil. He was ready for a brawl, and this uppity Negra would be just right for him, but then he looked beyond the man, and with a quick glance realized there were at least twenty others who wanted a part of the action. He slowly stood, hands on the table, then leaned forward and breathed deep. "If it was just me'n you, I'd tear you limb from limb," he growled.

Richards smiled and untied the strings of his apron. He started to remove it until Kavanagh interjected, "But with all your friends here . . ."

Richards continued removing his apron, and as he brought the loop over his head, he said, "Oh, don't let that worry you. They're just here to make bets. They won't interfere. They've been hopin' someone would dare to take me on so they could win back part of what they lost the last few times when they bet on the other guy." He dropped into a crouch, motioning with his hands for Kavanagh to come ahead.

With a roar that would make a bear with a sore tooth blush, Kavanagh tossed the table aside and started for the waiting Richards. Always one to bull his way through anything, Kavanagh depended on his size and strength to overwhelm any opponent. However, Richards and his father before him had had to literally fight for everything they had, and over the course of time with drunkards, fighters, and troublemakers, he had developed considerable skill at dealing with those like Kavanagh. As the big man rushed, arms outstretched, thinking to grab Richards and break his back, the innkeeper deftly stepped aside and brought up a sweeping right to bury it deep in the bully's mid-section.

Kavanagh exhaled with a whoosh, then bent over and stumbled forward, only to be tripped by Richards. The big man caught himself on the edge of a table. All the patrons had stepped back against the wall and were shouting encouragement and taking odds and bets by yelling across the room. Kavanagh turned, ready to grab Richards, but he was out of reach. With another roar, he charged, and this time caught the smaller man around the middle, wrapped his arms around him, and lifted him off the floor, arching his back bone as he sought to break the spine of the insolent colored man.

Richards had taken a deep breath and he smacked his forehead against the broad nose of the beast of a man who held him, smashing his muzzle across his face and splattering blood in every direction. The man released his grip, grabbing at his face as he bent over, only to be met with the knee of Richards, which snapped his head back and dropped him to the floor. He rolled to his side and used a nearby chair to get to his feet, then smashed the chair across the table-top and turned with a chair leg in his hand, "I'm gonna beat you to death with this!"

The innkeeper dropped into a crouch, grinned, and motioned with his hands for the man to come at him and try. Kavanagh stepped quickly, especially for a big man, and swung the chair-leg in a sweeping arc like a cricket bat, but Richards ducked under the swing and pummeled the bully with repeated blows to his ribs and side. Kavanagh staggered back, trying a backswing with the leg and missing again. Richards pressed forward with a left jab to his splattered face, followed by an uppercut that snapped Kavanagh's head back against the door-jamb. Pinned against the wall, Kavanagh took a beating from the scrappy innkeeper, who continued his onslaught with repeated punches to the belly. As Kavanagh tried to defend his middle, Richards spun around and brought his elbow against the jaw of the big man, then chopped at his head as he fell to the floor. When he hit the wood planks, his wind escaped with a gasp, and he lay still. Richards stepped back, motioning to two patrons, "Drag that *gentleman* out of here!"

12 / Hunt

"I think I'm gonna like these buckskins!" declared Gabriel as he stood near the campfire, showing off his new duds. Adorned with minimal beading at the yoke across the chest and short fringe dangling from the yoke and the sleeves and leg seams, the skins fit him well. The calf-high moccasins showed a simple pattern of beads across the toes and short fringe up the calves. His belt held a metal-bladed tomahawk, and he converted the boot scabbard that held his knives to one that hung between his shoulder blades by way of a double sling.

Ezra stepped into the light, running his hands across the soft buckskin and looked at his friend, "I *know* I like my buckskins!" His attire was comparable to Gabriel's, the only difference being the color and style of beading. They had met the mother-daughter pair who made the garments and were told the mother had made Gabriel's and the daughter had made Ezra's. "I think the girl did a better job than the mama! Lookee here at my beads, ain't they pretty?" He ran his fingers along the yoke of beads, looking down to admire the colors.

Gabriel chuckled, "That fits you just fine. You always were more of a show-off than me!"

Lucius looked from one to the other, "Never fancied buckskins myself. Ain't warm 'nuff in the wintertime! An' walkin' behind a plow? Nah. My woman keeps me outfitted just fine!"

"Now Lucius, these boys wanna be *frontiersmen* and *explorers.* They don't care 'bout walkin' behind no plow! Those outfits are just what they need for pushin' through the briars and thorns o' them bushes in the wilderness!" declared Hamish. He turned to his friend, "Don't you think so, Fred?"

"What do I know? I ain't never been much of a hunter! Oh, sure, I'd take some ducks, rabbits, and such, maybe an occasional goose, but I traded for most of my meat. I prefer the open fields and the rear end of a good plow horse to wanderin' around in the woods all day," answered the big bear of a man with the bushy red beard. The others looked at him, disbelieving, that such a big, barrel-chested man who appeared strong enough to pull the plow himself would have an aversion to something most thought to be a typical activity of a man.

"Well, speaking of hunting," started Gabriel, turning the attention from Fredric, "I think I'll take my horse and hunt a bit in the morning. While the river goin' is easy, I could probably get us a couple deer and meet you downstream a ways." He looked at Lucius with uplifted eyebrows as if seeking permission, or at least agreement.

"*Ja! Ja!* Sounds *goot!* We could use some fresh meat," answered Lucius, nodding enthusiastically.

Gabriel turned to Ezra, "I'll go tomorrow. You'll be here to load the other horses, and I'll meet you downstream." It was to become common procedure to offload their horses whenever they stopped for the night to give the animals time to graze and sleep without the rocking of the boat. Ezra nodded, "You startin' out early?" he asked.

"Umm hmm. Well before first light. I'd like to be somewhere along the riverbank to get a couple when they come down to water. If I get 'em early enough, I should be able to get them dressed out and ready to load when the boat comes close." This would be the first hunt of their river journey, and Gabriel knew it would take time to get a routine worked out on the hunting and picking up of the game.

Gabriel kept to the spit of land downstream of the confluence of the Beaver and Ohio. Staying close to the tree line, he used the dim light of the last quarter of the moon and the brilliant stars that sparkled from their ebony bed to guide him in the diminishing darkness. About five miles downstream, he came to what he was looking for, a break in the rolling hills that would probably hold a game trail used by the deepwoods animals as they came to water. He lifted his face to the cool morning breeze and grinned at knowing it came from the draw between the hills and would be at the back of any animals coming to water.

He stepped off his horse and glanced over his shoulder at the dim light in the east, then looked for the anticipated trail. His search soon yielded its bounty, and he led the big black into the thick trees and along the trail. He noticed fresh tracks, probably from the night before, and that the trail often went under long limbs that prevented him from riding the black up the trail since he would quickly be unseated by the big branches. When he was about fifty yards up the trail, he moved into the trees, finding a place about twenty yards off the path to tether his horse and ready himself for the hunt.

With the Mongol bow in hand, quiver hanging from his belt at his side, he walked further up the hillside, paralleling the track below. The darkness was slowly lifting its veil when he found a slight shoulder of rock that stood above the trail and would give him a good view of anything below. He nocked an arrow, holding it in place with his forefinger at the grip, and placed another readily at hand at his side. He had no sooner taken a shooting position than he saw a slight movement up the hillside. Thick foliage and dim light hindered him, but he watched as a young buck with small velvet antlers showing their first prong tiptoed his way through the brush. He stopped, one foot lifted, peering around for any danger. He had either sniffed or heard something that gave him pause, but a larger mature buck, also in velvet but with a broad rack and several points on his antlers, nudged him forward.

Believing the older deer to be the more skittish, Gabriel slowly drew the bowstring back, touching his cheek with the thumb of his right hand, sighted on the forward part of the buck's chest, and let the arrow fly. Without waiting for the strike, Gabriel deftly nocked the second arrow and, sighting quickly, sent the feathered missile to its intended mark. The big buck reared up, craning his head around at the startling pain, and fell to his side, kicking to try to get up. The smaller animal had lunged forward at the sudden jump behind him, but his lunge had been accounted for by the expert archer in the trees and the arrow buried itself in the ribs just behind his front leg, causing the young buck to fall forward. Unable to move his legs to catch his fall, he landed on his outstretched neck and chin. He too kicked momentarily, trying to rise, but was soon still and quiet.

Gabriel heard the retreating steps of at least one more deer, perhaps more, that had turned and fled back up the trail. He slowly stood, looking down at the two deer as he fingered the nocked arrow. He was ready to shoot again if necessary, but it would not be needful. He picked his way off the rocky promontory and down to the trail and laid his bow on the chest of the first deer as he slipped his knife from the scabbard and slit his throat for him to bleed out. He stepped back to the larger buck and repeated his action, then stood to look around. The sun had crested the eastern horizon, and he wanted to get the carcasses down to the spit of land at water's edge before the boat neared. He quickly went to his tethered black.

When he cleared the trees at the edge of the trail, he was surprised to see a man holding his bow as he stood over the carcass of the small buck. With long grey hair in two braids that rested on his shoulders, the wrinkled face of the man lifted in a smile to Gabriel. "*Hè!*" greeted the old man, lifting one hand, palm forward, shoulder high. He wore a breechcloth over leggings, but his wrinkled chest was bare.

"Hello!" answered Gabriel. He'd stopped in his place but

now continued forward, leading the black. He ground-tied the horse, turned to the man, and held out his hand for his bow. The old man, whom Gabriel guessed to be about sixty, extended the bow.

"That was fine shooting," he stated. "I've not seen a white man use a bow before, and that," nodding at the weapon now in Gabriel's hand, "is quite a bow. I've not seen one like that."

His statement was as much of a question as a comment, and Gabriel answered as he lifted the bow and looked at it, "It is a Mongol bow, used for centuries by the warriors in Mongolia."

Gabriel saw that the old man carried a bow of his own and a quiver with a few arrows. He asked, "You hunting?"

"Yes and no. It has been a long time since I walked in the woods alone, and I wanted to have some time without others around. My home is north of here, but the hunting is bad. When I was young, this," motioning with his head and eyes at their surroundings, "was my land." His eyes glazed as he looked down the draw to the waters of the Ohio. It was apparent to Gabriel that the man was remembering, and he said, "My name is Gabriel Stonec . . . Gabriel Stone," thinking it better to not leave his full name behind. He extended his hand in greeting.

The old man responded, "The missionaries call me William Henry, but among my people, the Lenape, I was known as Gelelemend or Killbuck." The two men shook hands and Gabriel paused, recognizing the name, "You were the chief of all the Delaware!" He stepped back, "Let me see if I have this right. You were the chief of the Turtle Clan. You succeeded chief White Eyes, but there was a division among your people and the bands under Captain Pipe and Buckongahelas allied with the British, but you didn't!"

The old man smiled as he sat down on a nearby rock, "You know these things well. Most white men only know they are white, and the natives are not, and are to be killed or run off."

Gabriel motioned with his knife that he was going to gut the deer and the man nodded his agreement. As he worked, he spoke, "Sadly, what you say is true. But just like among your people, some are good, some are not. But you said the missionaries call you William Henry. Does that mean you have become a part of their mission?"

Killbuck smiled, "No, what that means is that I have often thought about the Christians and what they believe, and I listened to the missionaries explain about Jesus. When I understood, I believed, and I asked Jesus Christ to be my Savior. So now I am a Christian!" he declared proudly.

Gabriel paused, turned to look at the man, and had nothing to say. While he had struggled with some things about the Christian beliefs, this man, in his sincerity and simplicity, had studied it out and readily and easily came to his decision to accept Christ. As he slipped his blade under the skin of the deer's belly and moved it toward the neck, he thought, *Why am I having such trouble understanding and accepting? Maybe I need to talk to Ezra more and get this settled sooner rather than later.*

13 / Boat

Gabriel made short work of field-dressing the deer. He put the two carcasses across the back of his black and started for the sand bar beyond the tree line. Killbuck followed as the men continued to learn about one another. "You will need to be watchful, Blue Jacket and his Shawnee are still hurting from the Battle of Fallen Timbers, and Buckongahelas wants to continue his fight. Some of these hot-blooded leaders still think they can defeat the Americans," avowed Killbuck.

"I understood Blue Jacket fled to Fort Miami, but the British wouldn't let 'em in, is that right?" asked Gabriel, leading the black from the trees. He looked upstream for any sign of the boat and, seeing none, he ground-tied his horse and walked to water's edge, looking for a likely landing spot for the boat.

Killbuck stayed with the horse, waiting for Gabriel's return. As he neared, the former chief explained, "That is true. Blue Jacket and his Shawnee had run from the general's charge, and when they could not get into the fort, they kept running." The old man laughed.

"Didn't General Wayne do more? I mean, I understood that his men destroyed a number of villages."

"Yes, and when he went to the main village of the Miami, Kekionga, he destroyed it and then built a fort that he called Fort Wayne," answered the former chief and leader of the Lenape.

He shook his head at the memory, "Perhaps that is why Blue Jacket and Buckongahelas are still angry. They lost more than warriors; they lost status and honor. The young warriors with them still go on raids, and the chiefs no longer control their people."

"Well, I've heard Washington is pushing for Wayne and others to get a treaty signed with both chiefs, and others as well. I believe you'll see all of 'em at a treaty conference soon," surmised Gabriel. He dropped the deer carcasses on the sandbar, loosened the girth on the saddle, and led his horse to a patch of grass near the trees. He looked at Killbuck, "So, could you use some fresh meat?"

The old chief grinned, "I am alone, but I am returning to my home. A portion of meat would be good."

Gabriel chuckled, went to the small carcass, split the hide along the backbone, and carved out a long backstrap of meat, smiling as he offered it to Killbuck. The wrinkles were drawn taut by the smile that stretched the man's face as he accepted the choice meat from the deer. He nodded his appreciation, then, looking past Gabriel, he said, "Your boat comes. I will go, and I will remember this time together with my new friend, Gabriel Stone."

"And I will long remember my talk with the great leader of the Lenape, Gelelemend," added Gabriel. The two men clasped forearms, and the old man turned and soon disappeared into the trees. Gabriel turned, waved to the boat, and motioned to the sandbar.

The sun had just cleared the treetops in the east as the flatboat nosed into the sandbar and Gabriel caught the line to make it fast. Only a few moments passed before Gabriel, his black, and the fresh meat were all aboard, and the two men on the sweep oars leaned into the long oars to pull the boat back into the current. Ezra helped Gabriel carry the carcasses into the cabin to be hung and skinned out. "Did I see you with somebody on that spit of land?" asked Ezra.

"Ummhumm. That was Gelelemend, also known as Killbuck. He used to be the big chief of all the Lenape people, but that was before the Northwest Indian Wars. Now, he's living alone, and helps the Moravian Missionaries at Salem."

Ezra leaned back, cocking his head to the side, "You don't say. Well, if that don't beat all!"

"But he also said we need to keep a sharp eye because a bunch of the young bucks who were with Blue Jacket and Buckongahelas has been makin' raids on the settlers and boats on the river."

"Have you told Lucius?" asked Ezra, groaning as he lifted the big carcass for Gabriel to tie it off to the overhead beam. The meat would hang and stay cool. With the hide removed, the men draped the meat with a thin cotton cloth and turned to leave. "You think we might be in for some trouble?"

Gabriel chuckled, "We've been in for trouble ever since we left Philly!"

"You know, my pa always said you were gonna be the death of me!" answered Ezra as the two men mounted the ladder to the top of the cabin. Fredric and Hamish had lifted the sweeps from the water and lay them along the top of the cabin, but Lucius handled the rudder oar, keeping the cumbersome flatboat in the center of the current. The other men would spell him as need be, and when more challenging currents required, they would use the "gouger," the short front sweep that helped them maneuver the boat as necessary.

Gabriel went aft to speak with Lucius, and as the man handled the rudder oar, Gabriel told him about his talk with the old Indian and his warning about the renegade young bucks from both Blue Jacket's Shawnees and Buckongahelas' Delaware. "So, he thinks some of those might try to take our boat?" asked Lucius.

"He did say they have attacked some settlers and some boats on the river," replied Gabriel. He looked upstream when something caught his eye, and his frown made Lucius look behind them. About three hundred yards away, a keelboat with a hoisted sail was gaining on their broadhorn. Lucius grinned, "It's a keelboat. They can make good time, especially with a sail. I thought about tryin' a sail on this boat, but I think they're more trouble than they're worth."

"Will it pass us?" asked Gabriel, surprised at the sight.

Lucius looked again, cocked his head to the side, "Probably

pass us by mid-day, if they don't stop along the way."

"Stop? Why would they stop?"

"Oh, some of 'em like to set up trade with the villages, depending on what they're carryin'. We often stop too. A lot of the goods we have aboard are for trading with the settlers and some of the Indians."

"I wondered about that. But after what Killbuck said, you still going to stop?"

Lucius chuckled, "Depends."

"Depends? On what?"

"If there are women and children, it is usually safe to stop and trade. But if all you see are men or warriors, not so much."

It was less than an hour when the keelboat drew alongside, staying about ten yards away, and slowly passed the unwieldy broadhorn. Several of the men lounged in the stern of the boat, and a couple lifted a lazy hand to wave as they passed. Standing at the rudder, the helmsman ignored the broadhorn, but a man standing nearby lifted his hand in a friendly wave. But when Gabriel saw the man, he scowled, remembering. He turned to Lucius and Ezra who stood nearby. "I saw that man at the boatyard, he was talking to Ebenezer, and they were looking at this boat and obviously talking about it or us."

"How can you be so sure?" asked Ezra.

"Did you see his nose? That big honker covers most of his face! And he had on the same waistcoat when he was with Ebenezer. When they talked, it was obvious he was angry at Ebenezer, but they were too far away to hear what was said."

"I'm sure it's nothing to be concerned about. Probably just a coincidence. Why, by the time we get to the Mississippi, we'll pass or be passed by more'n a hundred boats, and we usually see somebody familiar on at least one of 'em," explained Lucius.

"Coincidence? My father said there is no such thing as coincidence. There's always something behind whatever appears to be a coincidence. Besides, there's something . . . something that doesn't sit right. I feel it right here in my gut!" proclaimed Gabriel, putting his hand to his belt. He looked at Ezra, knowing his friend had what many called second sight. Ezra said it was hereditary from his long line of Black Irish, and their history with the Celts and the Druids. But Ezra looked at his friend wide-eyed and eyebrows raised, giving a slight nod that said both that he agreed, but they should keep silent about it.

Gabriel looked after the keelboat, wondering just what it was about those aboard, and especially the one man with the big nose. As he considered, his first thought was that he might have been sent by James Wilson, the father of Jason whom Gabriel had defeated in the duel. But Gabriel knew if the man had been sent by Wilson, he would not have been sent alone. If that was what the man was about, several of those aboard with him would be co-conspirators. But he thought it was something else, and perhaps it didn't have anything to do with him. He looked back at Lucius, "Do boats like this often get raided? You know, attacked, and have the goods stolen?"

Lucius looked at him from under scowling eyebrows, "What are you saying?"

"Nothing, just asking. Trying to figure out why that man

would be so angry when he was talking to Ebenezer and talking about us, and as they pass be wearing a big smile and waving. Maybe I'm just the suspicious sort, but it doesn't sit right with me."

Lucius looked at Gabriel, thinking, "Could he be after you?"

"I don't think so. Not that it wouldn't be possible; I did leave some enemies behind, but he doesn't appear to be the type. He seemed more concerned about the boat than me."

"We are carrying a considerable amount of whiskey. Since the rebellion over the taxes and such, not much whiskey has been shipped out. So, it might be tempting to some river pirates, I s'pose," answered Lucius. "And the rest of the cargo is pretty valuable also, so maybe."

Gabriel looked at the man standing at the tiller, "So, Indians are not the only ones we have to be on the lookout for, huh?"

"That's why we brought you fellas along, to protect us farmers!" proclaimed Lucius, laughing. But both men knew it was nothing to be laughing about.

14 / Settlers

Fifteen feet of prow stretched from the front of the cabin to the bow on the flatboat. Gabriel and Ezra decided to use the prow, which held the sandbox stove and the benches the men used as they gathered for their meals, but it would also be where they would roll out their bedrolls and stash their weapons and gear. Gabriel sat beside his saddle as he reloaded his pistols. As he used the screwworms to pull the balls and patches, he admired the handiwork of his father's cherished weapons. He had been surprised when he saw them in the holsters on his saddle when he left his home and family, but he knew his father wanted him to have the best, and these pistols were certainly the best. Sixty-two caliber, silver-mounted, over-under double-barreled flintlocks, they were beautiful and rare examples of the best of French handiwork. From the Louis XIV era, each barrel had its own flintlock mechanism, and the frizzen pans were so designed as to be almost waterproof. Ezra watched as Gabriel cleaned and reloaded the pistols, every move showing his love and care for magnificent weapons.

"Hey, let me see one of those," suggested Ezra, putting his own pistol down at his side. Gabriel handed the one he had just finished loading to his friend, and the man accepted it with care. He turned it over in his hands, admiring every detail, "All this, and they're accurate, too!" he mumbled as he held the pistol before him, sighting along the barrel.

Gabriel watched his friend, "I'm surprised my father let 'em out of the house. I remember when he brought them home; he had a velvet-lined mahogany case under his arm, and he was grinning ear to ear. When he lifted them out to show me, he held them like a newborn baby. And when we took them out to shoot, he was prouder'n a white peacock."

"With all this reloadin' and such, are you expectin' trouble? Perhaps from those fellas on the keelboat?"

Gabriel slowly shook his head, continuing his ministrations on the second pistol, "I'm not sure. I just know it got my hackles up when I saw that man, and, well, I dunno. I just figure it's better to be prepared, no matter what comes." He slipped both pistols into the holsters and took out his belt pistol to clean and reload as well. The smaller pistol, fifty-four caliber, was English made by W. Bailes and Company of a newer design. Although it too was double-barreled, it had only one flintlock mechanism, but two frizzens and pans. When one barrel was fired, the barrel assembly could be turned over, and the second barrel and frizzen was ready to fire. In a time when rifles and pistols were single shot, to have more firepower was a distinct advantage.

When he finished with the belt pistol, he laid it aside, picked up his Ferguson rifle, and cleaned, oiled, and reloaded it as well. Ezra had tended to his weapons, a belt pistol, a horse pistol, and his rifle, and was looking downstream. He stood for a better view and shielded his eyes, then frowned and turned to holler at the helmsman, "Lucius! There's some folks on the bank yonder. They're waving, and I think they want us to stop!"

"I see 'em!" answered the man, "Stand ready! Don't know what they're doin', an' I ain't stoppin' till I know!"

Gabriel stood and walked to Ezra's side, looking up and down the bank for any other sign of people or danger. He stepped to the prow and scanned the water and the sandbar, then looked at the people. He spoke to Ezra, "Looks like a man and a couple women. Man 'pears to be hurt!" They stood in the shadow of the timbered hills that had only a slight shoulder before the long sandbar at the confluence of Yellow Creek and the Ohio. The big river made a wide bend toward the south and the sun nestled at the edge of the trees up the valley of the Yellow Creek. Lucius had been watching for a good place to put in for the night, and the sandbar at the confluence suited.

Both Ezra and Gabriel had picked up their rifles and stood ready at the prow, watching the sandy bottom through the shallow waters. The three people were four, with one man, not seen before, seated beside the younger woman. As they neared, the older woman could be heard saying, "Oh, thank God! They're stopping!" She held a hanky to her face as she watched the boat come near. It pushed into the soft, sandy bank, and Ezra, hawser in hand, jumped to the shore and went to a big oak tree to tie off the boat. Gabriel jumped ashore as well, watching the people as he walked toward the small group.

"Oh, thank heaven, you stopped. We are so grateful!" cried the older woman. Gabriel smiled and nodded at her as he looked at the man beside her, obviously her husband. His rifle leaned against his side, but he held a bandage to his bleeding shoulder. His face was pale from loss of blood, and the other man, resembling the older but much younger, had a bandaged leg. He also had a rifle, which lay across his lap, and neither man showed any threat.

"What happened?" asked Gabriel, setting his rifle on its butt by his foot.

"Shawnee!" spat the man. "Burned us out. We lost everything!" he angrily declared.

"They hit us while the men were in the field, and there were at least twenty of them. But Jethro and James made it to our cabin, even though they were both hit. We fought 'em off for a while, but there was just too many!" explained the woman.

"They said they wanted to parley! So we listened. The one said his name was Tecumseh, and the other'n was his brother, Tenskwatawa. He said we could go but couldn't take anything with us! He said we were to tell others that any white man that came into Shawnee country would be killed. So, we had no choice but to leave. And 'fore we were a hunnert yards away, the barn an' house were afire. We had horses, a couple mules, a milk cow, couple pigs, and two fields planted an' growin'!

They took the horses an' killed and destroyed ever'thing else!" grumbled the man, "it took us the rest of the day to get here. Most o' eight, ten, miles," he added, using his rifle as a crutch.

Lucius and the others had joined the group, and he said, "Well, folks, we're gonna make camp here for the night. We've got some extra blankets for you, and we'll fix a good meal. When the fire's goin' and we can see better, we'll take a look at your wounds, I did a little doctorin' in the war, an' maybe I can help. You can come with us in the mornin'. We'll probably make Zanesburg 'fore nightfall, an' you can prob'ly get some help there."

"Thank you, Captain. You're a godsend!' declared the woman. "If you'll allow, my daughter and I would be happy to help with the meal fixin'?"

Lucius smiled, "That would be wonderful, ma'am. We haven't been on the river long, and we're already tired of our own cooking. Hamish there," nodding to the big Scot, "will get you whatever you need."

"By the way, Captain, I am Mrs. Ainsley," she nodded to her husband, who had sat down on the edge of the riverbank, "my husband, Jethro," and, turning to the others, "my daughter Amy and my son, James."

"Pleased to meet you, even though the circumstances could be better," began Lucius, then introduced each of the men before everyone stepped to his duties.

The spit of land at the confluence showed a wide clearing, where Gabriel picketed the horses. He chose to stay ashore with the horses and watch the trail that followed Yellow Creek, although he didn't expect any trouble from the Shawnee, he believed them to have accomplished what they wanted and had probably returned to their village. But he was still uneasy about the other perceived threats: those aboard the keelboat, and if there were any thugs on their trail sent by old Jacob Wilson. Given the vigilance of the horses, he preferred to stay near them, while Ezra would roll out his blankets atop the cabin for a better lookout of both the river and the camp.

Gabriel placed his saddle at the foot of a big hickory tree, straddled it, and leaned back against the ancient trunk to watch the horses graze and the stars come out. It was a pleasant evening, cool and calm, and Gabriel listened to the night birds and watched as the lightning bugs sent their staccato messages to one another. His thoughts turned to his home and his father and sister, and he wondered about their welfare. Ever since his mother had passed most of three years gone, his father had been restless, and his life seemed aimless. Although he tried to tend to his businesses and investments, he had long ago established a staff of managers and advisers who easily managed his affairs without his direct involvement. Gabriel had talked to his father at length about his holdings, but his father had explained they no longer held any interest for him. "Son, if I don't get out of bed for a month, everything will go on as usual, just as if I was in my office shuffling papers and looking over things." It was then his father explained something that had aroused Gabriel's curiosity, but he hadn't been able to find any answers until then. "My health is failing, and I don't believe I have much time remaining. What I have will be held in trust for you, and I trust you will take care of your sister. There is more than ample to last you the rest of your life, and then some." But the duel with Jason Wilson had changed all that, and now as he sat leaning against the big old tree, he thought he might never see his father again.

The sounds of the night that had been the unconscious background to his thoughts had suddenly gone silent. Gabriel looked at the horses, all with uplifted heads, ears pricked. They were looking past Gabriel across the creek. The sounds of the rushing waters had masked the approach of several riders, obviously Indian, wending their way along a narrow game trail that followed the creek to the big river. The rising moon gave enough light for Gabriel to make out the riders, most with headscarves wound around their heads, some with feathers or plumage. Others had metal armbands or neckpieces that shone in the glimmering light. One man in the lead had a cast-off British officer's coat, and a few wore buckskin jackets over their buckskin leggings. They carried a variety of weapons, rifles, lances, and war clubs.

Gabriel was in the dark under the long limbs of the hickory and watched as the line of warriors picked their way toward the mouth of the creek. He assumed these were the same Shawnee that attacked the home of the Ainsleys, but he was surprised they would follow them, having allowed the family to leave before destroying their home. Surely, they wouldn't be going back on their word unless the story as told by the Ainsley's wasn't entirely true.

15 / Zanesburg

Gabriel had all his weapons at hand, but chose to remain still and watch. The band of warriors reined up at the mouth of the creek and the leader gestured to two of his followers, who dismounted and examined the tracks by the dim light of the night sky. With the Ferguson across his back with the woven rawhide sling, Gabriel slipped the matched pair of pistols from their holsters and padded through the shadows to a point directly across the creek from the Shawnee. He watched as the two spoke to their leader, repeatedly gesticulating toward the opposite bank, where Gabriel lay in wait. He wasn't anxious to get in a firefight with a band of fifteen to twenty Shawnee, but neither could he let them come upon their camp unexpected. He stood behind a large oak, the gnarled branches giving him added cover but restricting his view somewhat. He held the pistols at his side, looking along the bank and tree line and planning his defense.

He saw the leader lift his hand to signal his followers as

he pushed his own mount to water's edge. Gabriel breathed deep, lifting the pistols as he stepped from behind the big tree. He knew he could not be seen in the deep shadows, but he also knew that would change as soon as flame stabbed from the darkness. He waited until the leader was midstream and took aim, not wanting to kill anyone, but just stop their attack. With both hammers at full cock, Gabriel slowly squeezed the first trigger, and the pistol bucked as it spat fire, lead, and smoke. Instantly Gabriel ran to his right to another tree and squeezed off another shot, seeing the leader frantically reining his mount around as the second round blossomed red on the chest of the man behind him. Again, Gabriel moved, back to his left past his first cover, lifted his left pistol and fired, then, taking three more steps to his left, he fired again. Jamming both pistols into his belt, he swung the big Ferguson from his back, eared back the hammer as he moved back to his right, dropped to one knee, and squeezed off a round that lifted another warrior off his horse. Two men were frantically splashing in the water, fighting their way to the bank, one floated face-down, and the leader, still astride his mount, shouted orders to his men as he led them back up the trail.

Before the lingering cloud of smoke dissipated, Gabriel had reloaded his rifle, and watched the band retreat. He was breathing heavily, still on one knee, when he heard Ezra, "What's happening?"

"Shawnee!" answered Gabriel, not taking his eyes from the trail as he reloaded his saddle pistols. Ezra was at his side, rifle before him, looking in the direction of Gabriel's nod. He saw the body in the water, another on the bank, but saw nothing of the band of warriors. "Prob'ly the same ones that hit the farmer's place!" surmised Gabriel, finishing his reloading. He stood, pushing the pistols behind his belt, and started back to his lookout and the horses. Lucius came to their side, asking the same questions and getting the same answers, but Gabriel added, "I just don't understand why they would say the family could leave, then come after them. It doesn't make sense, usually when a native gives his word, it's his bond. Now, if they were outlaw white men, I could understand it, but . . ."

"What makes you think treachery is subject to skin color?" asked Ezra.

Gabriel stopped, looked at his friend, and shook his head, "That's what I implied, isn't it?" He shook his head again, "You're right! Doesn't make any difference what color a man's skin is, he's just as subject to the thoughts and treachery as every other man." He slipped the saddle pistols into the holsters beside his saddle, then sat down and looked up at Ezra, "I don't think they'll come back, but if they do, I can see fine from here."

Lucius asked, "You sure you'll be all right?"

Ezra looked at the captain and chuckled, "He'll be all right. Didn't you hear that barrage he let fly?"

The captain frowned, "You don't mean all that shooting was from him?" he asked, nodding toward Gabriel.

Both Gabriel and Ezra laughed as Gabriel answered, "Yup, just me!"

"Weren't the Indians doing any shooting?" asked Lucius.

"Unless I miss my guess, Gabriel here didn't give them a chance to. Am I right, my friend?"

"You're right. It just didn't seem logical to let 'em."

They pushed off at the first hint of light, and once in the middle of the current, the men lifted the sweeps and joined the others at the sandbox stove as Mrs. Ainsley and her daughter Amy prepared breakfast for the crew. When Hamish relieved Lucius at the rudder, the captain joined the others at breakfast.

Mrs. Ainsley asked, "Do you think we'll reach Zanesburg before dark?"

"Yes'm. Shouldn't have any trouble getting there well before dark. I hope to do some trading with the folks there before we settle in for the night."

"How big a place is Zanesburg?" asked Gabriel.

"Oh, I don't rightly know. There's probably ten, twelve families, maybe more by now. Ol' Ebenezer Zane founded the place, although it was originally French territory. Zane claimed it with 'tomahawk rights' where a man can stake out a place by girdling the trees with his tomahawk, add his initials, and it counts as his. It used to be a fort, Fort Henry, but 'fore that, it was Fort Fincastle. They fought the Shawnee, Wyandot, and Mingo tribes, as well as the British." He chuckled at a remembrance, "Seems that when the British and some Indians laid siege to the fort, the people were runnin' out of ammunition. But the Zane family had some at their homestead, so ol' Ebenezer's sister, Betty, volunteered to run get it, seemed she was faster on her feet than any o' the men. So, she up an' ran from the fort right in front of the British an' their Indian friends, went to the house, poured the powder into a table-cloth, an' ran back to the fort. Them Britishers was shootin' at her all the time but couldn't hit her, she run so fast. An' 'cuz o' that powder, they saved the fort!"

Everyone had been held spellbound by the tale, and Gabriel was the first to speak up, "That's quite a tale. Is it true?"

Lucius frowned as he looked at the man, "Course it is! An' I got 'nother'n," he looked around, and as the listeners leaned forward, he began, "Before that siege, there was another one, this'n just by Indians, but the troops at Fort Vanmetre heard tell of it and they come under the command of Major Samuel McColloch. But the major got separated from his men, and the Indians took off chasin' him. He led the Indians away so his men could get to the fort. He took off up a trail on the mountain behind the fort, an' he didn't rightly know where he was, but he knew them Indians were hot on his trail. Of a sudden, he reined his horse off the trail, saw the fort down below, and kicked his horse into a run, and they ran right off that cliff an' fell near 'bouts three hundred feet down its side. When the Indians came up to that jump, they stopped and looked over, thinking they was gonna see a dead man and horse, but what they saw was that man ridin' his horse outta the trees and headin' back to the fort. And to this day, they call that place McColloch's Leap!"

Fredric had been listening attentively but leaned back and shook his head, "Can't be. Ain't no man nor horse can make a jump like that and live!"

Lucius looked at his friend with a scowl, "Tell ya what I'll do. When we get there, I'll take you out and you can look at the place. Then you can ask anybody round there the truth of the matter, and you'll find I have told the full truth! And I'll bet you a silver dollar on it!"

"You've got yourself a bet, and I will enjoy taking your money!"

With the storytelling over, the men returned to their stations atop the cabin at the sweeps. Gabriel and Ezra resumed their duties, watching for sawyers and sandbars while they stood in the bow of the broadhorn. Amy Ainsley came to Gabriel's side and asked, "Whatcha lookin' for?"

Gabriel looked down at the girl, noting that she had cleaned and fixed herself up a little, looking more like a young woman than a lost waif in the woods like she had before. He smiled, "We're watching for sawyers, submerged trees and such that could snag and damage the boat."

"Oh! Seen any?" she asked, smiling coyly up at the tall man beside her.

Gabriel guessed the girl to be about fifteen, old enough to be married, and quite attractive with dusky blonde hair, clear white complexion, and deep-brown eyes that seemed to show a touch of mischief. "Not yet," he answered, turning his eyes from her and back to the water.

"What happens when you do?"

"We shout the warning, tell 'em where it is, and if we have to, grab those poles yonder," nodding toward a pair of long, peeled poles that lay alongside the cabin, "and help push off."

"Ever fall in?" she asked, smiling mischievously.

"Not yet," answered Gabriel.

"Too bad, might do you some good," exclaimed the girl, smiling and turning away to return to her mother's side at the sandbox stove.

Late afternoon saw the boat nosing into shore atop a shallow rift and deep sandbank. Lucius was especially excited about the prospects of trade and jumped off the boat to pass the word they had goods to trade for pelts and more. Within the hour, several folks had come to the shore and waited for the trades to begin. When all was done, the boat was lighter by two barrels of whiskey, one of the Valentine stoves, three plowshares, two pigs, and several pieces of cookware. But their cargo hold was just as crowded, with bundles of furs and pelts from bear, elk, lynx, and wolves. Lucius and his partners believed they had done well and anticipated many more profitable trades before they arrived in New Orleans. But tonight should be a restful night for all, with no concern about an attack while they were docked near the settlement.

16 / Search

Morrow's Green Tree Tavern was the agreed-upon meeting place for the four men in search of Gabriel Stonecroft, but the only men at the corner table were Shorty and Hitch. They slowly sipped the tepid beer as they waited, light dwindling through the fly-specked window behind them. Hitch growled, "That blasted Kavanagh prob'ly got drunk and in a fight!"

"If they don't show up soon, we'll go on without 'em. Stonecroft is only one man, and he shouldn't be too hard to handle," answered Shorty.

"What about that Negra of his?"

"Ain't nobody gonna be bothered if there's one less colored man to be concerned about."

As they quaffed their beer, Warner Burns stepped through the door, paused as he surveyed the patrons, then, recognizing Shorty and Hitch, came to their table. As he seated himself, the maid brought a mug of beer and set it in front of the newcomer, smiled at him, and left. Shorty asked, "So, where's Kavanagh?"

"Left him," declared the usually tightlipped Burns as he reached for his mug.

"Would you care to elaborate on that?" asked Shorty, bringing a frown to Burns' face.

"Got'na fight," responded the man, giving a broader description of events than was usual.

"Should we wait for 'im?"

Warner Burns scowled at Shorty, shrugged, and chugged his beer.

Shorty ordered another mug for each and the three sat silent, save for some occasional grumbling, mostly from Hitch, while they waited for Kavanagh. Their restlessness did little to mellow their temperaments, and trouble seemed to be brewing as Hitch, tired of Shorty's gab, tried to aggravate Burns into talking. "What's with you, anyway? Is it 'cuz you're afraid of people that you don't talk?" snarled Hitch.

Burns scowled at the bigger man, shrugged, and finished his beer. Hitch tried again, "Ain't much of a fighter, huh? Maybe I'll hafta teach you a thing or two!" he goaded, clicking his mug against Burns'.

"Shut-up, Hitch, leave 'im alone. We don't need more fightin'! Save it for the other'n," cautioned Shorty. He looked up as a man entered; the dim lantern light showing little, but the size of the man told Shorty it had to be Kavanagh. He hollered, "Kavanagh!"

As he came into the light from the lantern hanging on the nearby post, the marks of the fight were upon him: swollen cheeks, blacked eye, cut lip, and knots on his head, one still showing blood. Shorty said, "Looks like you got waylaid!"

He mumbled through swollen and split lips, "Colored tavern, jumped me. After he ran out," pointing with his chin to Burns as he sat in the single remaining empty chair.

"Never mind that! We've got work to do!" Shorty leaned forward, drawing the others closer as he began to detail his plan. "Now, we know they're on a flatboat or broadhorn. Those things don't move fast at all, so if we cut straight west of here, we can hit Holiday's Cove and get us a boat. Whether it's a keelboat, longboat, or if nothin' else, a couple of canoes, any of 'em move faster'n a flatboat. So, it might take a few days, but we can hit 'em whenever we want, take ever 'thing on the boat, and get the reward for Stonecroft as well!"

"But if they're on a flatboat, there'll be more of 'em," whined Kavanagh.

"That ain't gonna be a problem. If we hafta get more men, we will, or we might just pick 'em off one at a time. There's plenty of places on that river where no one will know anything, and we can blame it on the Indians! But once they're floatin' face-down in the river, who they gonna tell?" chuckled the stubby boss.

What was four to five days on the circuitous river was only two days cross country for the gang of four. They had outfitted themselves well in Pittsburgh and trailed two loaded pack-horses as they came into the village of Holiday's Cove. The remains of what had been Fort Holiday sat on a slight knoll, and the scattered homes lay in a disarrayed manner, with one road that held a trading post, tavern, and stable. The men made for the stable and left the horses and gear with the stableman before going to the trading post. Shorty had made a contact in Pittsburgh who had referred him to the trader, and after being certain there was no one else within hearing, Shorty told the man, "Hoppy in Pittsburgh said you could help us."

"Ol' Hoppy, huh? What's that outlaw up to now?" asked the clerk, looking at Shorty with a suspicious frown.

"The usual no good, but he said you an' him was partners on a couple things, an' if anybody could help us, you could," stated Shorty, taking another look around to ensure their privacy. He leaned toward the counter, "We need a boat. There's somebody we're after that's goin' down the river on a flatboat, so we need somethin' that'll catch up with 'em."

"It'll cost' ya!" growled the man, uncomfortable with the four men in his small post. "Ain't had no keelboats through. 'Course, that could change, but you'd do better takin' canoes."

Shorty turned to look at the others, but with no response, he looked back at the trader, "No longboats or nuthin'?"

The trader chuckled, "I ain't seen a longboat on that river since I been here, an' that's more'n ten year! But if'n you wanna wait for a keelboat, he'p yourself. But I ain't sure I'd trust any of 'em. You might hire 'em, but most of 'em would just as soon take your money, knock you o'er the head, an' drop you in the river."

Shorty knew what the man said was true. Keelboats and their crews had a reputation for fighting and thieving, as many of the men who plied their living on the water were well known for their fighting ways. He thought about it for a moment, then looked at his men and back to the trader, "Let me see the canoes." Then looking back at the others, "Any of you ever handled a canoe?"

All three of the men nodded, and they followed Shorty through the back door of the trader's hut. He walked them to the river's edge, pointed at some brush nearby, and said, "There they are. Ain't been used in a while but should still be good. Got 'em from some Wyandot in trade."

Two large birchbark canoes lay bottom-up at the edge of the brush. The men looked them over, then turned the boats right side up and found several carved paddles. As they examined the insides, they carefully looked at each seam, which had been sealed with a blend of pitch and more, and the crafts appeared watertight. Hitch looked at Shorty and nodded, and the boss returned to the trader's hut to settle up.

As the trader tallied up the account, he added, "Now, a flatboat can make fifteen, twenty mile a day, dependin'. But with those birchbark canoes, you can almost double that, an' it's easier for you to travel after dark, too."

Shorty grunted his understanding, settled up with gold coin, and left the post. When he returned to the men, he instructed, "We'll spend the night here, prob'ly in the stable. Then we'll load up and get after 'im in the mornin'. But for now, let's get us somethin' to eat in that tavern yonder!"

As they took their meal, Kavanagh asked, "So, how we gonna know which boat's theirs?"

"That old man I had to pay for the info said there were only three other men on the boat. All three were farmers, two of 'em purty good-sized. Then there's Stonecroft and his Negra, and they got four horses loaded on the back of the boat. So, we just look for a boat with four horses and a colored boy, an' then we slit a few throats and take it all!" declared Shorty, slurping his stew from the bowl.

The other three laughed, then gobbled their food down, ogling the lone barmaid and anticipating their bounty from the reward and the goods on the boat. As they chided one another, they were in agreement that taking a boatload of farmers and some rich society fella and his Negra would be easy and mighty rewarding. Or so they thought.

17 / Visitors

A long day out of Zanesburg, with the Ohio river making a few twists and turns back on itself, and Lucius pointed the boat into the sandbar at the mouth of Captina Creek. While the men used the hawsers to make it fast, the captain stood atop the cabin and lifted a shofar to sound a call that echoed up into the valley of Captina Creek. Gabriel looked at the man, astounded at what he heard, and mounted the cabin to take a look. The captain hung the horn by a cord around his neck and lifted the rudder from the water to lock the long oar down.

"Just what is that thing, and what's all the noise about?" asked Gabriel, grinning as he walked to the captain.

The captain smiled and said as he lifted the horn, "This here's a shofar! It's a horn the Jews use for some of their ceremonies, I got it from a friend of mine from back in the old country."

"What'd you blow it for?"

"That's to let any settlers up that valley, at least them what can hear it, know that we're here an' ready to trade. Lotta folks listen for a horn, so they know there's a trader near," explained the captain. Gabriel and Lucius both turned as they saw another boat coming around the sharp bend upstream from their mooring, readily identified it as another flatboat, probably with settlers aboard but were surprised to see it was actually two boats lashed together.

"Well, I'll be a monkey's uncle." He turned to Gabriel, "I've seen 'em lash boats together on the Mississippi, but it's gotta be difficult negotiating some o' those bends here on the Ohio, bein' lashed together like that!" They watched as the pair of flatboats drew near and pushed into the bank behind and slightly upstream from their mooring.

"Howdy!" shouted Lucius, waving at the newcomers. There were women and children standing in the bow, chattering and waving until the boat grounded on the bank, jarring them all and making them grab onto each other or anything near. They laughed and watched men jump off and tie off the boats, dragging them closer into the bank to make them fast.

While Ezra and Gabriel offloaded the horses, others were making sizable camps near one another. The word had been passed that there would be music after the meal, and most were looking forward to a relaxing, fun time. Gabriel looked at Ezra, "I think I'll keep watch up there," pointing with his chin at a rocky promontory that overlooked the confluence of the waters and the valley beyond.

"Still think we might get a visit from that keelboat?" asked Ezra, leading his bay and the chestnut packhorse.

Gabriel spoke over his shoulder, "I dunno, maybe I was just bein' a little jumpy. But there's always the possibility of Indians."

"I s'pose, especially after the captain blew his horn!"

Gabriel chuckled, "Yup. That was like announcing, 'Here we are! Come get us!'" He shook his head, laughing, as they came to a broad green meadow with tall grass to picket the horses. Gabriel had made it a habit of throwing his saddle on the black just to transport his saddle, weapons, and bedroll to his look-out point, and after he led the black to the edge of the trees, he slipped his rig off, dropping it in the shade of a big tulip poplar. He looked back to Ezra, "I think I'll just stay here, or up there," looking to the promontory that stuck out from the surrounding trees and offered a view of both the valley and the river.

"Don't you want somethin' to eat?" asked Ezra, concerned for his friend. He was thinking as much about the promised party of music and more as well as the food.

"Aww, I got me some jerky and left-over biscuits from Mrs. Ainsley. I'll be alright."

Ezra lifted his head as he looked at his friend; it was unlike him to avoid social contact with others, but he was also known to occasionally be aloof and pensive. He shrugged his shoulders and turned back to the boat.

Gabriel called after him, "Enjoy yourself! And watch those ladies, I think I saw one eyein' you!"

Ezra laughed, "Ha! I ain't got any interest in romance!" he hollered back over his shoulder, seeing his friend wave as he started into the trees to mount the promontory.

Gabriel swung the saddle over his shoulder, holding it by the horn and carrying his rifle loosely in his other hand, occasionally using the butt of the stock to give him stability as he climbed the slope to the point. Once there, he dropped the saddle at the foot of an alder bush and turned around for his first look. He plopped down on the big flat rock and looked out over the spit of land and sandbar where the boats were tied off. He could see about a half-mile upstream, and a little less downstream, his view blocked by the nearby trees. He turned to look up the valley of the creek and saw the sun painting its farewell with a broad brush of orange and gold. He smiled and shaded his eyes as he looked at the valley floor, seeing the colors bounce off the creek's surface. To the south of the creek, he could make out a trail near the edge of the trees and saw four riders, at least one a woman, trailing two packhorses as they made their way to the confluence. He smiled, thinking they were probably settlers come to trade, and relaxed as he finished his initial survey of the area.

Most were finishing up their evening meal as the riders came into camp, hailing the group before they entered, and at the behest of those by the fire, the four riders came forward. Gabriel watched from his vantage point above the treetops as the riders were warmly greeted and asked to join the others. As Gabriel had suspected, there was a woman, actually two, that were among the riders. They had been riding astraddle, wearing britches under their skirts, but once on the ground, their skirts were lowered, and they mingled with the rest.

It was just a short while later that the fiddles, Jews harps, and harmonicas came out and the music began. The first song was a popular one from the Revolutionary War, called *The Rich Lady over the Sea*, and most knew the words, so they sang along.

> "*There was a rich lady lived over the sea,*
>> *and she was an island queen,*
> *Her daughter lived off in the new country,*
>> *With an ocean of water between.*
>> *With an ocean of water between,*
>> *with an ocean of water between.*
> *The old lady's pockets were filled with gold,*
>> *yet never contented was she,*
> *So she ordered her daughter to pay her a tax,*
>> *Of thruppence a pound on the tea,*
>> *Of thruppence of pound on the tea,*
>> *of thruppence a pound on the tea.*
> "*Oh mother, dear mother, the daughter replied,*
>> *I'll not do the thing that you ask,*
>> *I'm willing to pay fair price on the tea,*
>> *But never a thrupenney tax.*
>> *But never a thrupenny tax,*
>> *but never a thrupenny tax.*"

The song continued through four more verses that told about the events of the war and ended with a cheer from the singers. Soon a more jovial tune was begun, and couples were dancing by the light of the fire. Gabriel chuckled, thinking there was little difference between what he watched and what he had heard about the dances of natives in their villages and around their fires. As he watched, he heard the rattle of rocks below his point. He slipped his pistol from his belt and moved back near the brush, waiting and watching. Suddenly a voice called, "Gabriel? Gabriel?"

It was a slightly familiar feminine voice, and Gabriel answered, "Here," but still held his pistol at the ready. A hand reached to the edge of the rock, and then a face showed in the dim light, smiling. Amy Ainsley. Gabriel replaced his pistol and stretched out a hand to help the lass up. She held a covered plate in her free hand, and as she stood, she offered it to Gabriel. "Thought you might be hungry. I asked Ezra where to find you." She looked around, saw a flat-topped stone, and sat down, still smiling at a flabbergasted Gabriel. "Well, say something!" she declared.

"What are you doing here?" he asked as he sat cross-legged before her, uncovering the tin plate to see meat, potatoes, and a biscuit. He didn't hesitate as he started eating, and he looked at the girl, who sat smiling and watching. He swallowed and asked, "Well?"

"Oh, I came with the Willoughby's," she replied as if that simple statement explained everything.

Gabriel sloughed his shoulders, shook his head slightly, and asked, "Where's your family?"

"Oh, they stayed at Zanesburg. When I met Sarah Willoughby and she asked me to come along, I did!"

"What did your folks say about that?" asked Gabriel, slightly confused.

"Not much. They always favored James, and Pa thought girls were a bother and not good for anything, so he was kinda happy I was leavin'." She smiled and leaned forward, "How's the meal?"

Gabriel scowled, "The meal's fine, thank you. So, your folks are still at Zanesburg?"

"Ummhumm, after James pulled his stunt, I didn't think it would be too safe to stick around anyway."

"Stunt? What stunt?"

"You know, when the Shawnee attacked. They let us go, but when they set fire to the house, James took a shot at 'em, killed one, I think. Then they took'n off after us. We ran the horses to ground and had to run afoot till we came upon you'ns."

Gabriel huffed, shook his head, "So that's why they came after you! I wondered about that."

"Ummhumm, that's just the way James is, never thinkin' and always blowin' his top! I'm glad to be shut of 'im."

"So, what are you going to do?" inquired Gabriel, between bites.

"Oh, you know, find a fella, get married, have kids, make a home. You know, just like all the other womenfolk," she paused, looking at Gabriel with a mischievous grin, "how 'bout' chu? Wanna get married?"

Gabriel's shock made him spit out the food, then, glaring at Amy, he said, "Married?! No! I don't wanna get married! We don't even know each other!"

"Didn't think so, but I thought I'd ask. Ya never know till

ya ask, right?"

"Uh, I guess so. But don't you think you should at least get to know a man before you start talking marriage?"

"Well, the pickin's kinda thin, and folks don't always have the time for a real courtship," she declared, looking at Gabriel with her head cocked to the side, "'sides, you're a mite on the skinny side."

The party finished with the group singing *Amazing Grace* and *When I Survey the Wondrous Cross* together. When they turned in for the night, each one knew they would probably never see the others again and goodbyes were said, but the time had been enjoyed by all.

18 / Discovery

"That fella that came with those two women to trade, he was sayin' they saw some bison not too far from here. Said it's 'bout ten miles downriver. There's two streams, and one's bigger'n the other. First one's called Sunfish Creek and the second one's called Opossum Creek. He said them bison have been stayin' around Opossum Creek, 'tween there and the bend in the Ohio." Ezra had come to Gabriel's lookout once the doin's broke up to share what he had heard.

"You don't say? Well, I've always had a hankerin' to try a nice thick buffalo steak, haven't you?" answered Gabriel.

"Ummhumm, but from what I hear, tryin' to field-dress one o' them big boys is not a one-man job. You think the captain would allow both of us to be gone on a hunt?"

Gabriel grinned, "Why don't you just start by askin' him if he's ever had a buffalo steak? From what I've heard, if a man's had one, he won't pass up a chance for another one." He leaned forward, "We'll head out before first light. If we move right along, we should get there about the time they're movin' around and having their breakfast."

Ezra grinned, nodded, "See you at the horses in the mornin'."

With Lucius at the rudder, Hamish and Fredric leaned into the long sweeps to pull the boat from the sandbar. With the current pushing the stern around, and the men putting all their weight to the long oars, the boat pulled free and was soon underway. They moved by the dim light of the long grey line that lay upon the eastern horizon, barely showing over the tree-covered hills along the Ohio. Lucius looked back, seeing the campfires blazing on the shore and knowing the people they had sung and danced with were taking their time and enjoying breakfast before taking to the water. It was unlikely they would catch up again.

The hunters kept to the trail that followed the river at the tree line, cutting in and out of the timber that occasionally stretched to water's edge. It was an easy traveling path, and they made good time. The sun was barely peeking over the treetops on the eastern bank when they came to the first creek.

"This looks like what that fella described as the Sunfish," declared Ezra, standing in his stirrups to look upstream of the shallow waters. "He said the crossin' was easy just this side of that bend yonder," pointing to the west and upstream. "Looks to be less'n half a mile."

"Lead the way," answered Gabriel with a wave of his hand.

"He said it's 'bout two miles cross-country to the Opossum

Creek, and the bison're s'posed to be thereabouts," explained Ezra.

Gabriel looked at the sun and back at the hills, "Reckon we'll get there 'bout the right time. I've not hunted bison before, an' from what I understand, they take a mite of killin', so we'll need to make sure of our shots."

"Reckon that'll be decided by when and where we find 'em. But what with your .65 caliber and my .58 caliber rifles, we should be able to get at least one on the ground. If not, maybe we better stick to fishin'!"

"Fishin'? I don't remember ever seeing you fishin'!"

"Ain't got the patience," declared Ezra, chuckling.

They followed a dim game trail that wound through the thick woods but took the easiest way toward the smaller creek. Probably used by deer, maybe some elk and any bison nearby, it rode the shoulder of a ridge overlooking a draw that was thick with brush, too thick to move through. When they broke from the trees, they were overlooking the small stream, "I'm guessing that's the Opossum Creek." Gabriel stood in his stirrups to look up and down stream and spotted a bend in the creek and a meadow just beyond. He pointed it out to Ezra and in whisper tones, "That looks like a possibility. Looks like a wide draw with more grass 'tween those knobs, too." He dropped into his saddle, looking to his friend, "From what little I know, bison aren't like deer and elk; they prefer open places to the woods. What say we go up to that bend, cross over, and see 'bout huntin' on foot?"

Ezra nodded as Gabriel led off, following a narrow trail

along the shoulder of the ridges and paralleling the small creek. He kept looking to the meadow, searching for movement, but seeing none, pushed his black into the water to cross to the meadow. Once across, Gabriel stepped down, whispered to Ezra, "You hold the horses here. I'm gonna look for sign." He handed the rein to his friend, and with rifle in hand, walked slowly along the edge of the brush, searching the area for any sign of buffalo. He saw tracks of deer, one set of larger and more splayed tracks that were elk, but none were fresh. Crossing the low neck of the meadow, he watched the tree line for movement, but nothing stirred. At the far edge was a game trail that led from the draw that bent around the closest knob of a hill, and there were several sets of big tracks, bigger than any he had seen. He knew they were near some bison. He bent down to examine them closely, noting all the tracks were headed back up the trail into the hills and the area that appeared to hold a higher meadow. He stood, looked around, and returned to the horses and Ezra. He spoke softly, "There are several sets of fresh tracks, all heading up into that draw and valley yonder. Let's leave the packhorses here, and we'll ride on up thataway," pointing with his chin to the south branch of the valley. Once free of the packhorses, he mounted up and looked toward the upper valley, then pointed to the left, "I'll take this slope up to that ridge," then, pointing to the right, "you take that trail yonder, work your way to the top of that ridge, then we'll work around toward each other. If they're not in the open, we can push 'em from the trees and get a shot." He looked to Ezra, "Think that'll work?"

"Sounds good to me. See ya in a short while!" he declared as he gigged his horse toward the trail.

Gabriel smiled, and with gentle knee pressure, started his black up the slope. He soon topped out on the ridge, looked around, and chose to ride the crooked ridge as it followed the contour of the valley below. Moving in and out of the trees he often stopped, sometimes dismounting, to get a better look at the upper meadow. Nothing moved except the leaves in the breeze, and they weren't hunting leaves. He mounted again, starting along the ridge but watching for any sign the bison had crossed over, yet seeing none.

He stopped, stretched, and leaned on his pommel to look around at the wide vista beyond the ridge. He was on a point of land that the Ohio River bent around, coming from the north and turning almost due west before pointing due south again. He started to move on when something caught his eye at river's edge. He leaned over his pommel, craning for a better look below, and saw what he had feared for several days, the keelboat. It was moored along the north shore, and barely visible from his point as the trees along the bank stretched toward the river. He quickly looked around, realizing he was skylining himself, and stepped down, leading the black to a nearby sycamore. With rifle in hand, he stepped back toward some brush and dropped to one knee, looking not just at the keelboat, but searching the trees and trails below for any movement.

As he looked, he spotted several men walking along the trail that kept to the riverbank and moving upstream toward the river's bend, all carrying rifles. He scanned the area upstream of the men where the river bent around the bluff, noting the usual lee-side sandbar and a shoulder bluff that held the trail, and he immediately guessed what the men were planning. He quickly went to his black pulled him around to go back down the trail, and just before he dropped off the ridge, he searched the far meadow and ridge for Ezra.

He thought he saw movement, so he stood in his stirrups and gave the shrill repeated cry of the red-shouldered hawk, their oft-used signal to one another when in the woods. He paused, waiting, and the answering cry sounded. He gigged his horse down the trail and broke into the meadow just as Ezra entered the grassy flat. Gabriel waved him near and said, "We've got a problem! I just spotted the keelboat, and the men are getting ready to set an ambush!"

Ezra's eyes grew large, "Where? How many?"

"Just around the bend where the river turns around this hill behind us. There's maybe ten or twelve men with rifles that I could see. There might be others across the river. We've got to warn the boat!"

"You're right, but . . ."

"You've got to do it, Ezra. I know where they are, and if we do it right, we can get 'em in a crossfire and give them what they're wanting to give us!"

"All right, I'll go see if I can flag 'em down!" He paused, looking to Gabriel, "Would it be better if I get on the boat or come along the trail from this way?"

"Either way, but don't load the horses, they might catch a

stray bullet, and we can always come back for 'em!" suggested Gabriel.

Ezra grinned, grabbed up the leads of the packhorses, and started down the creekside trail at a canter. Gabriel started back up the same trail, picking his way to the top, planning on cutting through the timber before dismounting and approaching the ambush on foot. He was already picturing where he would go and how he would make his own attack as the adrenaline rose and his breath quickened. He had felt this way many times before and knew there was something within that craved the battle, something that made him think of himself as a warrior who carried the heart of ancients, a heart that determined his destiny and forged his future.

He touched the knives that hung from the thong at his back, as well as his pistol at his belt, and those in the holsters beside his pommel. He thought of his bow and his rifle and smiled the grin of a death angel bringing retribution upon the forces of evil. A chuckle escaped his chest and rumbled from his lips as he spotted a place to tether his horse and prepare himself for battle.

19 / Battle

Although he carried his Ferguson, Gabriel anticipated using his bow and the pistols in the close-quarter fighting he believed would take place. Stealthily picking his way through the trees, he angled his path toward the point of the bluff, determined to intercept the attackers. He knew their attention would be on the river and they would not be expecting anyone from the hillside, but one slip, one turned stone, or any sound would make him instantly vulnerable. But this is what he and Ezra had practiced for years as they sought, as youngsters do, to sneak up on one another in the woods, and they had learned to move as quietly as the natives. His moccasins made the task easier, feeling every step before placing his weight.

He started to move to another tree when movement caught his eye. Less than twenty yards below, a man was scooting around for a better seat as he waited for the ambush to begin. Spotting one man, it was easier to find the others. Lined out, each finding cover that would obscure them from the river, and with an exclusive line of fire, their positions were readily located by Gabriel. They were in sort of a zig-zag line following the contour of the land, with trees behind them and brush before them, but nothing that significantly hindered Gabriel's access. He dropped to one knee, looking under the branches of the black willow, planning his moves. He would wait until their attention was captured by the appearance of the boat, knowing those aboard would be within the cabin, shutters closed, and ready to return fire.

They were well within range of his pistols, so he laid one beside the willow, moved to his left behind the furthermost shooter, propped his rifle against a maple, then moved back along the line, laying another pistol beside another black willow, then moved again. With only his bow and belt pistol at hand, he looked back along the line of trees that would be his cover, checking the trail for any hindrances, and moved back into the trees. Taking a position well above the last few attackers, he had a clear view of three men along the firing line. He settled in to watch. He could not see the bend of the river and would not see the boat as it appeared, but he knew the line of men were watching the water and each other, and the first appearance of the boat would cause the men, now relaxed and waiting, to react and ready themselves for the fight.

A sudden burst of gunfire sounded, but it came from the other side of the river. The rattle of rifle fire echoed across the river, and Gabriel realized the plan of the attackers was to push the boat to this shore by an attack from across the river. They would come nearer these attackers, and if they still prevailed, the rest of the men were waiting downstream with the keelboat. The initial attacked had spaced their shots and it was easy to identify the return fire from the boat, but Gabriel knew the blistering fire of a close attack might be overwhelming to those aboard. He stood beside the sycamore, drew back the arrow, and sent it to its first target. Without any hesitation, he nocked another arrow and let it fly, then a third. He paused to look, saw three men down, and heard another shout, "Indians! Indians!"

Gabriel chuckled as he ran to his pistol and fired as another shooter turned. The bullet struck him in the throat, taking a chunk of neck out the back as the man fell into the brush. His second round took a man in the shoulder as Gabriel jammed the now empty pistol behind his belt and went for the second. A bullet clipped the leaves by his head as he dropped to his belly, grabbed the pistol, and took a quick shot through the brush, hearing the unmistakable sound of a bullet hitting flesh. He came to his knees, looked below, saw a rifle stab flame, and felt the heat and sting of the bullet at his shoulder, but quickly aimed and fired just as the man started to reload. He saw the bullet strike his chest and spin him around, dropping him into the brush.

Gabriel rose to a crouch, ran to the maple where his rifle waited, and dropped to one knee, looking for a target. Three shooters were firing at the boat, their attention captured by the return fire and their reloading, and Gabriel carefully took aim at the furthermost attacker. He squeezed off his shot, and the big Ferguson rifle bucked as it spat smoke and death. He quickly dropped it to his side, turned the trigger guard to open the breech, dropped in the ball and then the powder, and spun the guard to close the breech. He lifted the rifle, saw the first shooter was down, and swung toward the second. Within less than a minute, he had fired and reloaded four times and scored a hit with all four bullets. The smoke from his shots clung to the trees, marking his position.

He scrambled back to his right just as two bullets cut bark on the maple. He stood behind a tall tulip poplar, hugging the furrowed grey bark of the wide trunk. He paused, sucking air, trying to calm himself, then took a quick look below, spotted another shooter starting to rise, and he snapped off another shot, hitting the man in the forearm, making him drop his rifle. The man looked up at Gabriel with wide, frightened eyes and started to yell to another, but Gabriel grabbed the pistol from his belt, and in one swift move, brought the double-bar-reled weapon to bear and squeezed off both shots. They took the man in the face, stifling his warning. Gabriel stuffed the pistol back behind his belt with the other two and dropped to his knee behind the tree to quickly reload the Ferguson.

He heard boots stomping through the brush coming to-ward him and he looked up to see a man charging, his rifle at his side as he bellowed his threat, "I'm gonna kill . . ." His charge was stopped when Gabriel's tomahawk made one turn before burying itself in the man's forehead. A grunt came as the man stared cross-eyed at the handle and he dropped to his knees, then fell on his face, the impact driving the blade deeper. Gabriel finished reloading the rifle, looked around for any other threats, and started reloading the pistols. He relaxed for just a moment, breathing deep as his shoulders lifted, and he slowly stood for another look.

The firing had stopped, and Gabriel looked to the water to see the slow-moving flatboat gliding on the placid current, no one moving. He gave the shrill cry of a red-shouldered hawk and paused, waiting. Finally, he heard Ezra's answer and saw a shutter on a side window open a crack. Gabriel stepped from behind the tree, motioning downstream, trying to warn those aboard about the keelboat. With another survey of the trail that had held the shooters, Gabriel quickly descended the hillside, working his way to the bank as the boat put into shore. The spot chosen was shielded by overhanging sycamore and willow, and Gabriel caught the hawser to make the boat fast. Ezra jumped ashore, "What're we facing?" he asked. Lucius leaned over the side to hear.

"The keelboat is moored just below. You probably saw it, but how many men are there is the question. There were ten or twelve here, plus those on the other side, so there could be as many as a dozen more at the boat."

Fredric's voice came from the prow, "There's a canoe crossin' towards the keelboat. Must be them that shot at us from the other side!"

"Did any of these get away?" asked Ezra, nodding toward the trail that held the attackers.

"I dunno, maybe. I was havin' to move too fast to keep track."

"So there could be as many as fifteen or twenty there?" asked Lucius, nodding toward the keelboat.

Both men looked that direction, then at one another as Gabriel nodded, "Could be."

"Look! They're leavin'!" shouted Fredric. He stood tall in the bow, pointing. "Guess we showed them!" Then the man was knocked backward as blood blossomed at his chest, and the boom of a rifle came from the brush. Everyone dropped behind cover, but Gabriel took to the brush after the shooter. When he broke out of the thicket at a run, he saw a man fleeing, brought up the Ferguson, and snapped off a quick shot. The man stumbled and fell, face in the dirt, unmoving. Gabriel made a quick scan of his surroundings and returned to the boat. Lucius and Ezra were bending over Fredric, then Lucius looked up at Gabriel, shook his head somberly to tell him the man was dead.

Ezra came to the side of the boat, "We need to get the horses 'fore we go much further."

Lucius stood at his side, "We'll stay here 'til you get back with the horses. We need to bury Fredric anyway."

Gabriel looked to Ezra, "You work along that trail yonder and pick up the weapons and such. Maybe cover 'em over some, but be careful; you might find some wounded and dangerous. I'll go get the horses."

When Gabriel returned, they loaded the horses, choosing to leave them on deck for the night since they had their fill of fresh grass. The men would stay aboard as well. Ezra said, "Got a few rifles, nine of 'em, and some pistols and knives to trade. One fella had crawled off into the brambles to die, and I didn't wanna go after him. So, maybe that fella on the keelboat won't be so anxious to mix it up with us again."

Gabriel shook his head, "I wouldn't sell him short. Just don't know about his kind."

20 / Stockade

Ezra looked up to see Gabriel approaching aboard his long-legged black stallion but with only his bay gelding in tow. He stood at the rail of the boat, hands out to his sides, palms up, and shrugged. Gabriel understood the unspoken question and grinned, "I left 'em back yonder. Thought we might need 'em." Lucius came to Ezra's side, looking at Gabriel, and he explained, "I jumped some buffalo outta the trees, shot one, and thought I could use your help to dress him out a little."

Ezra laughed, "Now if that don't beat all! We ride all over these hills, can't find a bison anywhere but kick up a bunch of trouble, and you go for a leisurely ride and take one without me."

"Not entirely. Your horse was there!" chided Gabriel, watching as Ezra gathered up his rifle and gear to join him.

It was late afternoon when they returned, one packhorse pulling a travois with the heavy hide of the bison, and he carried some meat aboard his pack. The other packhorse was loaded with meat, with more behind the saddles of the men.

Lucius and Hamish helped with the unloading of the meat, hanging it all in the cabin, and Gabriel and Ezra rubbed down the horses and got them aboard. Lucius said, "I'd like to get at least a couple more miles downriver before we put in for the night. Don't like those boys in the keelboat knowin' where we are, and I figger on puttin' in on the other side. Maybe find some cover for the boat."

"Good thinking, Captain," answered Gabriel. "Me'n Ezra won't be as good as Fredric, but we'll spell each other on the sweeps, if that suits," he suggested. Both men knew Fredric would have to be replaced if both Gabriel and Ezra left the boat at the Mississippi, but it was left unsaid. "Is there another stop 'fore long?" he asked.

"Couple days, we'll come to Picketed Point Stockade. Quite a few settlers there, so we might do some tradin' an' such. Stopped at Fort Harmar, 'cross the Muskingum before, but it ain't no more. But the Stockade is growin'. They built it to protect the settlers from the Indians during the war, but now that Wayne showed 'em what for, there will probably be lots more come."

Gabriel and Hamish were at the sweeps when Lucius motioned to the east bank toward the point of a long narrow island. He hollered, "We'll take that branch and moor behind the island!" The men nodded, and lifted the oars from the water, letting the helmsman control the boat with the rudder alone. They faced the back of the boat, looking at the captain, but turned to watch their approach to the narrow channel. The current pulled at the boat, and Hamish dropped his oar in the water and pulled, using all his weight, slowly turning the bow. He hollered to Gabriel, "Drop your oar in and push!" Gabriel immediately responded; swinging the blade of the oar toward the front of the boat. He dropped the blade into the water, leaned into it, and pushed, digging his moccasins into the rough wood as he fought against the long oar.

Finally out of the stronger current, they lifted the sweeps from the water and let the captain work his way with the rudder. Ezra stood at the bow, guiding their landing, and once the prow touched the muddy bank, he jumped to shore, hawser in hand, and tied off the flatboat. He caught the thrown rear hawser and tied it off to make the boat secure, then jumped up on deck and asked, "We gonna offload the horses?"

Gabriel looked at the bank and the thick trees and brush, "And do what? There's no place for them to go. We'll just give 'em some grain; they'll be happy!" He climbed down the ladder from the cabin top and spoke to his friend, "Let's get some axes. The captain wants us to camouflage the boat with some branches an' such, just in case those river pirates come lookin'."

With early starts, good weather, and swift currents, two days saw the boat nosing into the north bank of the Ohio just upstream from the confluence with the Muskingum River. Once moored, they had to climb the bank to see the settlement. "There she is, boys, Picketed Point Stockade! Looks kinda imposing, doesn't it?" asked Lucius as he started toward the fort, waving for the others to follow.

Set back a good distance from the Ohio, it was nearer the

banks of the Muskingum, and covered just over four acres. Double gates faced the four men as they neared the picket-post walls. With blockhouses at each corner and sentry boxes, or turrets, overhanging, it was well fortified. Men could be seen moving in the sentry boxes, and as they approached the gates, the guards signaled to open, and one was pushed out just enough for their entry.

Lucius led the way and greeted the men at the gate, "Howdy! I've got a boat down yonder and wanted to talk trade. Who do I see?" he asked.

"Well, we got us an emporium down yonder," answered the guard, nodding his head to the interior of the fort, "but if'n you're wantin' to just trade with folks, we can pass the word too."

"Thank you, sir, I would appreciate that. You can let folks know we've got lots of goods: whiskey, pigs, chickens, flour, stoves, pots, and such, and we'll trade for just 'bout anything. Now, we'll go along and see the emporium, then we'll be back at the boat."

"I'll do that!" answered the guard and pulled the gate closed behind them. "Say, you ain't seen no Injuns, have you?"

"Several days back we came on some Shawnee, but since that time, just some river pirate scoundrels."

"Oh, that's good. Well, uh, I mean, uh, you know!" sputtered the exasperated guard, relieved at receiving no news of Indian attacks.

Lucius grinned, nodded, and turned to go to the emporium. As they entered the structure, dim light showed through one dirty window, but still revealed several shelves, mostly empty of goods, a gun rack with one rifle, and a man leaning on his elbows on a plank that bowed between two barrels. He looked up as they entered, "Howdy! What'chu need?"

Lucius chuckled, "It would appear that I should be asking you that question!" he said, motioning to the empty shelves.

"What'chu mean?" grumbled the man, standing up and looking askance at the visitors.

Lucius stepped forward, "We're just in from Pittsburgh, and we've got a boatload of goods to trade. Interested?"

The man grinned, "Yeah, but I ain't got much to trade. What'chu got?"

Lucius leaned with one hand on the plank counter, "What'*chu* got?"

The trader laughed, "I've got some pelts and some tanned hides. Reckon that'd be 'bout all you'd be inter'sted in."

"I'll look at the pelts and hides. I've got staples, chickens, pigs, pots, stoves, and whiskey. And," turning to Gabriel and Ezra, "these fellas have some rifles and such."

The trader looked to Gabriel, eyes shining, and said, "I can always use rifles an' such." He turned to the back and called over his shoulder, "Lemme get the hides," then paused and pointed, "There's a bundle o'hides there, but I'll get the rest."

It was just a short while until Lucius and the trader had settled on the hides and peltries, and he brought a two-wheeled cart around to load the bundles and take them to the boat. The trader had agreed to come see the rifles before settling on a price, knowing Gabriel and Ezra were not interested in peltries. But when he came from behind the building, he held out something to Ezra and asked, "What'chu think of that?"

Ezra looked at what the man held, then up at him and said, "That's a warclub!"

"Ain't it, though? Traded that off'n a soldier with Wayne. He took it off an Injun he said was a Potawatomie. That there's ironwood; don't know what them stones is, but that there blade looks like it come from one o' them Spanish axes or whatever."

Gabriel said, "Halberd; they were called halberds. With an axe blade on one side and a piercing point on the other, and yes, that does look like a blade from a halberd."

Ezra took the warclub, hefted it, stepped back and swung it in an arc as he spun around. He grinned at Gabriel, "Remind you of somethin'?"

Gabriel chuckled, "Yeah, you and your Viking warclub you tried to brain me with!"

Ezra looked to the trader, "You wantin' to trade this thing?"

The trader grinned, "Let's see what'chu got."

At the boat, where several people waited, the trader and Lucius swapped goods as agreed, then Lucius turned his attention to the settlers. The trader stepped on board to have a gander at the rifles and other gear and to dicker about a trade with Ezra. When all was said and done, they traded three rifles and molds and possibles pouches, two pistols and three knives, for the war club and a handful of coins. The trader went away happy, cart loaded to overflowing. While Lucius and Hamish tended to the trades with the settlers, Gabriel and Ezra offloaded the horses and took them to grass, Ezra returned to get supper started.

As dark began to settle over the land, Gabriel returned with the horses, choosing to have them on board and easier to guard for the night. As he stepped around the cabin to join the others in the prow of the boat around the sandbox stove, he was surprised to see a young couple sitting by the stove and talking with the others. Lucius looked up, "Here he is now! Gabriel," he started, standing and motioning to the young couple, "This is Rufus and Persis Putnam. They'll be joinin' us for the trip downriver. Seems they plan on returnin' to Europe and were needin' a way to New Orleans, where they hope to book passage on a ship. Rufus here'll help with the sweeps and Persis's a good cook, so she'll make sure we eat well."

Gabriel stepped forward, hand outstretched, shook Rufus' hand, and nodded respectfully to Persis. He was immediately taken by the beauty of the woman; she had long, flowing black hair, deep, dark pools for eyes, and a smile that showed white teeth. Her bonnet hung to her back, but the ties were in a bow at her throat, and her dress was well-tailored and quite fashionable, which Gabriel thought surprising this far away from any city. She curtsied and dropped her eyes, holding a hanky at her mouth that did little to hide her smile.

Usually very affable and talkative, all Gabriel could do was nod and say, "Pleased." He stepped back and seated himself beside Ezra and listened as Lucius continued his conversation with Rufus. Ezra looked at his friend, chuckling as he dropped his head to look at his coffee cup. The others had finished their meal, and Gabriel reached for the pot to pour himself a cup of coffee, catching the girl looking at him with a coy smile parting her face. He turned away and sat again beside Ezra, "We movin' out early?" he asked, confounding his friend, who answered, "Don't we always?"

"Y-yeah, I reckon," he stammered, lifting his cup for a drink. "I'll let you take first watch. You can wake Hamish, and I'll take the last watch," stated Gabriel, rising. "I already threw my saddle up top, so I'll roll out my blankets at the rear of the cabin." He walked around behind the others to climb the ladder to the cabin top. Once atop, he paused, shook his head at his frustration, knowing he had never been stirred by the presence of a beautiful woman like he just had, and he thought, *Get a hold of yourself! She's married! And besides, you don't need to be gettin' interested in no woman! You're goin' to the wilderness, remember?*

He walked to his gear, arranged his saddle and weapons for quick access, and rolled out his blankets. As he stretched out, he took a deep breath and looked at the stars. He looked for familiar constellations, noted Ursula Major, then the smaller constellation, and traced the line with his outstretched hand and finger to find the North Star. He smiled at the thought of using that very beacon to guide Ezra and him across the wilderness of the West, where there were new lands to be discovered and many adventures awaited. He chuckled, *Now I'm soundin' like a kid, a kid with dreams of the big wide world. Oh, well, maybe it is!* His eyelids grew heavy and he started to slumber, but two deep, dark eyes smiled at him as he dropped off to sleep.

21 / Castle

"No, there ain't no castle there!" responded Lucius, leaning into the rudder sweep.

"Then why do they call it a castle?" asked Gabriel, always wanting to learn.

"I dunno, maybe 'cuz it looks like a castle with those walls an' all. You'll see what I mean in just a short spell. It's just beyond that island there," he said, pointing with his chin to the tree-covered island to the left of the main channel.

"Been there long?" asked Ezra. Both he and Gabriel had been lounging atop the cabin while Rufus and Hamish were tasked with the sweeps.

Gabriel wanted to stay shy of Persis, still very uncomfortable in her presence. When the men spelled one another for their nooning, she had prepared a fine meal of bison steak, biscuits with honey, and asparagus. She was friendly and tried to engage Gabriel in conversation, but he quickly excused himself on the pretext of checking on the horses. Now back atop the cabin with the others, he talked to the men about their next stop.

"Oh, not long. Five year, maybe. They got 'em some fine bottom-land farms around the castle, produce good crops. Seem to be able to grow most anything." Lucius pointed to the east bank of the Ohio, "Been a fella wantin' to get a settlement started there on the Virginia side, 'n I heard tell he wants to call it Newport. But ain't much there yet."

As the flatboat nosed into the bank, the trees that lined the shore hindered Gabriel's view of the structure, although further along, he could see the end and corner of an unusual picket wall. He craned around to see the wall that leaned out over the edge of the bank of the river but seemed quite secure in its setting. As Ezra shouted, Gabriel's attention turned back to his task at hand and he threw the heavy coiled hawser to his friend on the shore, standing between some bushes and before a band of tall sycamore trees. Ezra quickly tied off the hawser to a strong tree and looked to the boat for the rear hawser just as it landed at his feet, accompanied by the laughter of his friend and oft-times tormentor, Gabriel.

Ezra waited while Gabriel lowered the heavy planks for offloading the horses and stabilized them in the bank with a sound kick, then stepped aside as Gabriel led the big black off. He jumped on the planks to bring the others. Once all four horses were ashore, they led them to a wide, grassy meadow, picketed them soundly, hobbled the two saddle horses for good measure, and returned to the boat to go with the others for a good look into the Farmer's Castle.

Although it looked like a frontier fort, the sole purpose of the fortification was for the protection of the settlers during the Northwest Indian War. But the war had been short-lived, and the fort-like structure provided protection as well as community. "The original settlers called this place Bell-prairie, but after they built this," said Lucius, with a wave of his arm to take in the massive structure, "most got to callin' it that castle for them farmers, so the name kinda stuck!" Lucius was leading the group on their self-guided tour, and he prided himself on his knowledge of the founding of the new territory. "It's 'bout a quarter mile along the front there, and a couple hundred feet wide. Them pickets are 'bout ten feet high, split oak, and sunk four feet in the ground. There's thirteen blockhouses 'bout twenty feet square, and the second floor's bigger, as you can see. Hangs out o'er the lower level for defense. They shoot through them little slits there at anybody comin' 'round without a invite!" He started toward the open gate, "They ain't got no store or emporium, but one fella kinda turned his blockhouse into a tradin' place. We'll go say howdy and see if'n there's any folks fit for a trade."

As they entered, it appeared there was one long street going straight through to the other gate. The blockhouses rose on either side and pickets stretched from house to house. A walkway sidled around the houses on both sides, and the roadway was rutted from wagons traveling through on wet days. Dogs lazed about, barely lifting an eyebrow at the passing of visitors, and a few chickens scattered before them, clucking to announce their arrival. One yellow cat hung on the pickets, claws buried deep, as he meowed his complaints through the spires of the sharpened pickets. An occasional window with curtains pushed aside told of vigilant women, busy at their work about the house but watching everything within the palisades.

After Lucius made their presence known with the trader, they walked through to the end of the street and out the other gate. "Friendly bunch, ain't they?" asked Gabriel.

"Well, most o' the men are still in the fields. Trader said it's been kinda a dry year and they got more bugs and weeds than usual, makin' more work for the men. But, the women, now, that's what happens when things are all walled up like that 'stead'a out in the open. Folks stick ta' home, don't get out and talk. Ain't healthy, I'd say."

As they walked around the fort to return to the boat, Gabriel considered what Lucius had said about the people, and he thought it was much the same with the city. People stayed in their homes or businesses, visited only with those at their workplace or with their families at home, and socializing was at a minimum. But in the smaller communities, farming communities, people make it a point to meet at church or other community activities, like barn-raisings, and to help one another. He smiled as he thought about it, realizing that was what he preferred—the small community. Or, truth be known, he preferred the solitude of the wilderness, but there was much to be said for being around others, like Persis with her deep, dark eyes that held mystery and wonder.

He shook his head just as they came to the path to the mooring and started down the trail, passing others coming up the embankment path. Four men, one after another, pushed their way past, one bumping shoulders with Gabriel with a grunt and a warning, "Watch yo'sef!" he grumbled. Gabriel scowled but didn't reply as he noticed the man behind the bully. Big, splotchy nose and dressed like a gentleman, with a waistcoat, ascot, and greatcoat over britches and spatterdashes, and the familiar scowl he had seen at the boatyard in Pittsburgh. This was the man with the keelboat that had attacked them, but now was not the time for a confrontation, not with a woman in their midst.

As soon as they stepped back aboard, Gabriel called Lucius aside, "Remember the man I mentioned that I saw aboard the keelboat that passed us?"

"Yeah, what about him?"

"I was certain the keelboat tied off below where we were attacked was the same one, and now I know it. Those men that passed us on the path?" nodding back to the trail up the embankment, "He was one of them."

"With the pirates?!" asked Lucius, perplexed. He leaned to the side to look past Gabriel to the path, knowing the men were long gone but having to look to be certain. Then, turning back to Gabriel, he asked, astounded, "He was with the pirates? And here?"

"That was him and no mistake!" declared Gabriel.

Lucius gave it a little thought, then asked Gabriel to gather the other men together for a conference. "We need to put our heads together 'bout these pirates," he stated, lifting his shoulders as he took a deep breath.

As the five men gathered by the sandbox stove, seating themselves on the benches and pouring some hot coffee, Persis excused herself to go into the cabin away from the men, giving them the opportunity to discuss things together. Lucius began, "Look, Hamish and I have the most to lose, but you two," nodding to Gabriel and Ezra, "have been with us since the outset, and you're part of all this now. But this is gettin' to be more than we bargained for, an' I ain't sure quite what to do. Gabriel said he recognized that fella from the keelboat that attacked us, and with him and his crew bein' here, I'm certain they'll try again." He dropped his head as he rested his elbows on his knees, shaking his head from side to side.

"Cap'n, like you said, me'n Ezra have been with you since the outset of this journey, so we're stickin' with it. Those pirates, as you call 'em, tried to kill me'n Ezra, and that just doesn't sit too well with us. So, I'd like to see this through, and see what we can do with those pirates." Gabriel leaned forward, looking from man to man, "Now, here's what I'm thinkin'. First, Lucius, if we could get a couple more men here at the castle to come along with us? You said you wanted to pick up a couple extra hands anyway for when me'n Ezra leave, 'n that would be a start."

"Yeah, I should be able to find a couple men, there's always some wantin' to go to New Orleans for somethin' or other. Say, and maybe we could . . ." The conversation and planning continued. They paused when some of the settlers came to do some trading and Persis needed to fix the evening meal. Gabriel and Ezra went to check on the horses, and after the trading was over and supper was done, the conspiring and planning resumed. But this time Persis hung around, listening, pretending to be busy with clean-up from the meal, but Gabriel noticed she was quite attentive, and it wasn't just to look at him, although she did enough of that as well. As their planning and sharing began to slack off and dusk was fading into darkness, Gabriel stood and stretched, "I'll take first watch, even though nothin' much should happen while we're here. Ezra and I will bring the horses back aboard, and after my watch, I'll wake Hamish," nodding to the big man. "You can wake Ezra for the last watch."

"Wait a minute, I can take a watch just like the rest of you!" declared Rufus adamantly.

"Not tonight," answered Gabriel, "You need to stay with your wife for now. Maybe later on down the river, you can take a turn."

Rufus and the others smiled and laughed together, leaving Gabriel frowning and confused. Rufus stood, nodding toward Persis, "She ain't my wife! We're twins! She's my sister!"

"Sister?!" responded Gabriel, stunned.

Rufus walked to Persis' side and put his arm around her, "We've been twins all our lives!" he answered, somewhat smugly and a little mischievously. "I've wondered why you were avoiding her. Now we know!" he said, nodding toward the others, who were also surprised at Gabriel's astonishment. Lucius chimed in, "I thought I told you that when I introduced them?!"

Gabriel cocked his head to the side a little, looking at the captain, "No, you did not! All this time when she looked at me, I was thinking she was a little indiscreet for a married woman. Now I know, she was just being friendly, not flirty!"

"Flirty!" spat Persis, hands on her hips as she glared at Gabriel. "Why you pompous . . .!" She couldn't finish her thought as the others laughed, leaning back, even clapping their hands. They all had a good laugh at Gabriel's expense, and she couldn't help but join in with the others.

22 / Combine

It wasn't unusual for several flatboats to be moored together, usually for fellowship and mutual protection. The more
boats and people, the greater the safety. Yet there were some
flatboats that weren't inhabited by families of settlers, or
even farmers or tradesmen going downriver to market their
goods. It wasn't unusual for a gathering of boats to be because
a minister of the gospel had a boat for his church and would
seek to minister to the travelers. Others might be showboats
full of entertainers, or galleries for photographers or artists or
printers, others were floating brothels called gunboats, some
called wanigans that were cook shanties, bunkhouses, and
supply boats, and there were shanty boats on which families
lived permanently. So, when Lucius saw a conglomeration of
flatboats, he steered wide, suspecting the possibility of pirates,
for they often attended such gatherings, seeking new victims.

Curiosity has a way of stealing a man's better judgment,
and Gabriel and Ezra were no exception. Wisdom nagged at

the backs of their minds as they kept to the far side of the boat, but when the ruckus from the crowd snagged their attention, they stepped around the corner of the cabin for a better look. The largest of the boats that caught their eyes was moored in the middle of the pack, and a small group was gathered in the prow, tuning up their instruments. Gabriel recognized a clavichord, a viol, two violins, and a lute.

He was also surprised to see several fipples. He turned to Ezra, "That's a clavichord! I've only seen one before, and that was at a recital at the university!" He chuckled at the remembrance of the harpsichord-like instrument and what he thought was a rather tinny sound.

Ezra asked, "What are those others? That one looks like a violin, but bigger."

"That's a viol, and that other long-necked thing, that's a lute. It's an Italian instrument. I'm bettin' those folks are gypsies. They're the only ones I know of who are that musical! They make good music, and I'd like to hear 'em play. Those other things are called fipples, and they're recorder types. They blow into 'em, and they make a whistling kinda sound."

Lucius overheard their conversation and leaned over, "But we're not stopping. Places like that are where the pirates like to scout for their next targets!"

Dusk was dropping as they passed near, and some of those on the big flatboat saw them and started waving them over. One shouted, "Come on an' join the fun! We're gonna be dancin' soon!"

Lucius stood tall and cupped his hands, "Can't! Got sickness aboard! Might be the pox!"

At the word "pox," all the action on the big boat stopped, and the only motion given was for them to pass on by, to which Lucius nodded his head. "You folks have a good time now, y'hear!" He leaned over to speak quietly to Gabriel and Ezra, "Maybe that'll give any pirates somethin' to think about 'fore they come after us!"

Their boat showed little resemblance to what it had been before their stop at the castle. With logs stacked at the side of the cabin top and at the gunwales, and rifles positioned all around, it looked more like a pirate's craft than a trader. Two more crew had been added, a father-son duo who gladly signed on for the trip to New Orleans. Judson Whitehall and his son, Boxley, had planned the trip for some time. After Judson lost his wife to ague, he had lost interest in the farm and Boxley, a young man of sixteen, had a strong case of wanderlust. Both were good-sized men, standing about six feet, the father at least forty pounds heavier and more muscled than the lean young man. But the boy's willingness to scrap had earned him some scars and skills, while his eagerness to learn added to his limited wisdom. Both showed themselves to be hard workers and readily took to their duties.

Lucius nodded at the common mooring of the broadhorn boats, "That there's what they call Forked Run. It's a twisting valley what follows the creek bottom and leads back up into some good farmland. If them others weren't there, I'd stop an' blow my horn an' get some tradin' done. But there's another good place 'bout five miles yonder, an' we'll put in there." He lifted his eyes to the lowering dusk, "The moon'll be up soon, an' we can make it there and put in all right."

As they rounded the big bend that pointed the river southward, the rising moon bounced its gold off the ripples of the river, making them appear to be a chorus of sparkling nymphs dancing on the water. Lucius pointed the long boat to the sandy shore on the Virginia side and let the current slowly nudge her into the muddy bottom. Rufus and Ezra jumped into the shallow water, each one bearing a heavy hawser, and stretched them out to tie off the heavy boat. That done, both men trudged back to the boat since Lucius had said everyone would stay aboard this night. He was still concerned about the river pirates, and rightly so since the occurrences of boats being taken had increased since his last trip downriver.

Daylight came all too soon, but the awakening lights were less obnoxious than the blast of Lucius' horn that told the settlers of the presence of a trade boat. But Persis was already busy at the sandbox stove, with a big pan of sourdough biscuits baking, and a pan of eggs and another of pork belly cooking atop the plates. Gabriel stretched as he walked close, yawning widely and rubbing his eyes, "I'm not used to sleeping this late! I guess all that work Lucius put on us fortifying this boat wore me out more'n I thought!"

"Maybe a good breakfast will do wonders for you," answered the smiling Persis.

Gabriel thought she was looking extra pretty in the morning glow that came from the sun kissing the treetops on its early climb to the blue. He asked, "So, you and Rufus are heading across the pond, huh?"

She smiled, "Yes. The rest of our family is in Herefordshire, England, and they have many holdings there, farms and such. Although we have some family in the Salem area, we were never close with them, and we would like to visit our family's roots and see the 'old country' our father often spoke of, plus Rufus would like to study for the law at Oxford."

"And you? Are you interested in more education? Or something else?"

"I'm not sure. I've always been fascinated with city life, although we never had the opportunity to be in the city very often. And the possibility of seeing New Orleans holds some interest for me. I've only agreed to go with Rufus because of his interests, not mine, but with no other family here, I don't have much choice," explained Persis, busy at the pans on the stove.

Gabriel wanted to ask why she hadn't married but bit back the question as she turned to face him with her own question.

"So, what is so interesting about the West that has you leaving home to go a-wandering?"

It was an obvious redirection of the conversation, so Gabriel responded, "From the time I first began to read, I was always fascinated by the unexplored regions of our world. As I grew, so did my curiosity and desire to learn more about this great land, and to explore it firsthand. Circumstances were such that the opportunity came sooner than expected, so Ezra and I decided to follow our dream!"

"Dream? Both of you had the same dream? That's odd. You

two are nothing alike!" she observed.

Gabriel chuckled, glancing to the cabin top where Ezra still reclined on his bedroll, obviously awake but enjoying the lazy morning. "We're more alike than you think. We've been friends since childhood, and often was the time we wandered together in the woods, imagining what it would be like to explore the unknown." He chuckled again, "He keeps me grounded."

"Grounded?"

"Yeah. I'm usually the one with the wild ideas and gettin' into trouble, and he's the one who bails me out or makes me think twice about things. He's a well-educated man; his father is the founding pastor of a sizable church in Philadelphia, and like most children of preachers, he has his streak of wildness also."

"So, the two of you do make quite a pair," summarized Persis, grinning at the thought.

"You could say that," answered Gabriel as he reached for the coffee pot.

He looked to the shore to see a small group of men coming toward the boat, lifting their hands in greeting as they neared. "Hello, the boat! You a trader?"

"That we are! We've got staples, chickens, pigs, whiskey, and more! You ready to do some tradin'?" hollered Lucius from atop the cabin.

"That we are! Say, you wouldn't happen to have a stove to trade, would you? Kinda like that'n on your boat there?" shouted the larger of the trio.

"Sure do! Got a couple to choose from. What'chu got to trade?"

And the trading began. Hardly had the first three settlers finished their dealing than more began to dicker and deal with Hamish and Lucius, while the others lifted and loaded the goods for the settlers. Gabriel and Ezra chose to keep the rest of the weapons aboard in anticipation of another attack and busied themselves rolling barrels of whiskey and other goods and loading hides and farm goods aboard. By mid-morning, all the trading was done, and they pushed off just in time to see two of the boats from the previous night pass by, but none were friendly to the boat with the suspected pox aboard.

23 / Canoes

The party was well underway, the women from the gunboat were mixing with the crew members from a keelboat, and several couples from the other boats had paired off for the square dance. The caller ordered, "Allemande left with your left hand, bow to your partner and shake their hand," as the four couples in each square stumbled through the steps. Only a pair of the by-standers noticed the two canoes slip in between the big broadhorn and that of the settlers.

Shorty Steinberg cautioned, "We're just here to find out about the boat with Stonecroft and his Negra, so don't go causin' a ruckus! And that especially means you, Kavanagh!"

"Do you see them women? That there redhead's my kinda a woman!" declared the big Kavanagh by way of answering the order of the short Steinberg. He punched Hitch on the arm, "There's enough for both of us, Hitch! Hehehe," he declared, pointing at the dancers. "An' lookee there! That little un's just right for you, Shorty!" There was a short woman, somewhat chubby and a little older than the others, but she was still attractive. The boss just nodded, "Remember what I said; don't go spoilin' everything just cuz you wanna woman!"

After unloading their gear, they pulled the canoes up onto the bank and overturned them atop their gear, then headed to the boat with the dancing. The women were willing to trade partners and dance with all the available men, including Hitch and Kavanagh. Warner Burns stayed off to the side but readily partook of the available drinks. Shorty stood near the big crate that made up the bar and spoke with another man standing nearby.

"Was that you that came in with the canoes?" he was asked. The inquiry came from a well-dressed man who looked the part of a city gentleman, but his rather obvious proboscis that was hard to ignore. Shorty looked at the man, trying to look into his eyes, but found it difficult and chose to look toward the dancers as he answered, "Yes, me and three other fellows are on the chase for an escaped slave. He was last seen aboard a flatboat, and we're anxious to find him. You haven't by chance seen a colored man among the group here, have you?"

"No, can't say as I have. But there's no tellin' what or who might be hiding aboard these broadhorns." The man extended his hand, "I'm Ian Soames, and you're?"

"Oh, sorry. I'm Shaheen Steinberg, but I also answer to Shorty, for obvious reasons."

"So, this Negra you're looking for, is there a reward?" asked Soames somewhat nonchalantly.

"A small one, but the bigger bounty in on the man that

took him. A white man by the name of Gabriel Stonecroft is wanted for murder."

"Murder? Must be a bad one, then."

"No, not necessarily. Seems he killed a prominent citizen in a duel, or so they say, and the reward is offered by the dead man's father, a former member of the Second Continental Congress and well connected in other circles," explained Shorty, shading the truth for his own purposes.

"And you and your men expect to catch up with him and take the two of them from your canoes?" asked Soames, chuckling at what he considered an absurdity.

Their conversation was suddenly interrupted when a fight broke out in the middle of the makeshift dance floor atop the cabin of the flatboat. Kavanagh and a man from the keelboat wanted the same woman, and the disagreement quickly came to blows when the man called Smitty let loose a haymaker that knocked Kavanagh to his back. Stunned, the big man scrambled to his feet, pulling his long-bladed knife from his boot and dropping into a crouch, arms wide and knife moving from side to side, "I'm gonna gut you for that!" declared Kavanagh as the two men warily circled one another. A shout came from the side, "Smitty! Here!" and a knife was tossed to the fighter. He reached for the knife as it was tossed, giving Kavanagh a sudden opening, and the big man lunged, blade edge up, and plunged the knife into the man's lower gut. He used his left hand to knock Smitty's arm down, preventing him from catching the thrown knife, then stepped in close, grabbed the man's shirtfront, and pulled him into the knife blade.

Kavanagh grinned and pulled the razor-sharp blade up, opening the man's gut as his eyes flared with fear. The knife-wielding Kavanagh growled into the man's ear, "I said I'd gut you, and I did!" He yanked so hard on the knife that the blade bit into Smitty's ribs and Kavanagh had to jerk it to free it from the bone as the body dropped to the floor, blood and guts pouring out of the ripped gut wall. Kavanagh stepped back, wiped the blade of his knife on his pants leg, and slipped it back into his boot.

The crowd had gone silent, staring at the dead man and Kavanagh. The killer shrugged. "I told him I'd gut him, but he didn't believe me!" He walked to the makeshift bar and demanded a drink. Two men dragged the body off the cabin roof and threw it into the river, then dusted off their hands and returned to the dance floor as the music began again. Within moments, the frivolity continued without any more thought of the dead man.

Ian Soames turned to Shorty and said, "That was one of my men he just gutted!"

Shorty grinned, "Ummhumm, and that was one of my men who did the butchering!" He chuckled, "And you were saying something about us taking the men aboard a flatboat?"

"Judging by the action of your man, I'm guessing you're not too particular about how you take that slave and his friend, am I right?" asked Soames.

"The man paying the reward wants only the white man's head in a bucket, so no, we're not too particular," answered Shorty.

"This reward, big enough to split?"

"Five hundred dollars, mebbe a little more." He wasn't about to tell him about the additional five hundred offered for Stonecroft's head in a bucket, nor for the extra one thousand promised to Shorty personally.

"I might know something about your quarry, and since we're now another man short, we could use some more men. We are in that keelboat yonder," nodding to the only keelboat moored at the bank.

"You said, 'another' man short. Have you been in a scrape with our runaway?" asked Shorty.

"Perhaps. A flatboat that is carrying some cargo we want surprised us when my men tried to take it, and we lost some of our crew. I believe there was a colored man aboard, but we haven't been up close, and he might not be the one you want. We've been waiting for the right opportunity to try again, and we need to recruit some more men. Interested?"

"What do you know about this boat?" asked Shorty.

"It came from Pittsburgh. Some farmers with a considerable load of whiskey and a couple of men with horses."

"One of the horses a big black, nice horse?"

"Sounds right."

Shorty grinned, certain they were talking about the same man. He knew Soames would attempt to get all the information about the reward from him and then try to kill him and his men to collect the entire reward themselves, but two could play that game, and Shorty believed himself more than capable of double-dealing with the best of them. He extended his hand, "Here's to a mutually beneficial partnership!"

Soames chuckled and offered his hand to seal the agreement. Then the two men refilled their glasses to toast their deal. Shorty looked at Kavanagh, "Join us for a toast, Kavanagh. This is our new partner, Ian Soames!"

"Partner!? Ain't *my* partner! I ain't splittin' my share with nobody!" growled the big man.

"But he has that keelboat yonder, and there might be a few other prizes taken that can be shared as well! Besides, he knows where Stonecroft is!"

24 / Rapids

Rufus and Hamish manned the sweeps and Lucius was on the tiller when the boat moved into the current again. Although Judson Whitehall and his son Boxley spelled those on the sweeps, Gabriel took a turn at the tiller, but only under the close watch of Lucius. He was being groomed for the gouger or front sweep. Ezra moved about on the prow, always watching for sawyers, sandbars, and eddies that could drag the boat into the depths of the river, and of course, special vigilance was given to any passing keelboat or any flatboat they encountered. Persis was happy with her duties at the cookstove and was often heard humming a tune. She would sometimes break out in song. She had a velvety contralto voice, and the men would often pause in their work to listen to the girl serenade the creatures of the passing forest.

Between turns at the tiller, Gabriel slipped down for a cup of coffee and a few moments of pleasant company with Persis. She smiled up at him as she poured his coffee, "So, you've come down to the level of the rest of us, I see."

Gabriel scowled at her, "What do you mean?"

"Well, you are obviously from higher society and the wealthy class, but none of us are, so. . ." she answered, shrugging.

"Obviously? And on what do you base your conclusions?" inquired Gabriel, believing they were starting some kind of game of wits or something.

"It is easy to tell that you are well-educated, and you walk as if you own the world, yet you are friendly enough and don't separate yourself, at least not intentionally. So, I suspect your family is prominent, probably wealthy, and of considerable influence."

"And you? Your family name, Putnam, is more recognizable than is the name Stonecroft. After all, your father and your uncle were both generals in the war and distinguished themselves, yet you consider my family and me, of which you know very little, to be prominent."

She sat down, looked up at Gabriel, and let a slight smile tug at the corners of her mouth, "You're right. I know next to nothing about your family, and I was quick to judge, forgive me."

Gabriel relaxed, sat down across from her, and said, "Well, to be honest, you were mostly right. However, the reason Ezra and I are here is to spare my family any possible retribution from another very prominent and vengeful family. You see, I was in a duel, and the other fellow did not choose to follow the proper manner of the *Code Duello*. As such, I had no choice but to defend myself, and he was killed."

"So, you believe his family will seek retribution?"

"Most assuredly. His father has been known as a very vindictive and ruthless man. I have no doubt that there are bounty hunters on our trail as we speak."

"You mean to say he has placed a bounty on you?" asked a very shocked Persis.

"He's done it before with other perceived wrongs, so, yes, I believe he has."

Persis looked at the man before her, seeing him in a very different light. She was a little befuddled at the mixed feelings that were stirring within. "So, that's why you and Ezra are going to the unexplored regions beyond?" she asked somewhat quietly and reservedly.

"Yes and no. We are going to the West because we have always dreamed of and planned on going, not because we are running away. However, we hadn't planned on going quite this soon, but circumstances being what they were, it seemed to be an opportune time."

She smiled as she checked the stew on the stove, then opened the drawer to check the biscuits. Then turning back to Gabriel, she said, "Well, sometimes God works in mysterious ways, His wonders to perform!"

Gabriel chuckled and sipped his hot coffee, "Now you're sounding like Ezra!"

The rest of the day saw them make good progress. Lucius was quite adept at keeping the boat in the swiftest part of the current. They passed a pair of flatboats that had put into the shore for their nooning, but Lucius preferred to keep moving as long as there was daylight. By late afternoon, with about two hours of full daylight left, Lucius nosed the boat in at the point of a long strand of shore that showed the beginning of a long bend of the river. He hollered down to Gabriel, "We're puttin' in here just to offload your horses! There're some rapids around that bend, and it would be easier on them and us if they weren't aboard!" Gabriel waved his understanding and started to the back of the boat but paused to look to Persis, "Would you like to ride a spell and help me take the horses downriver?"

She smiled, nodding, "Let me change my skirt, and I'll be right there!"

As Gabriel ducked under the rudder sweep, Lucius said, "Just head through that run yonder," pointing to a dip in the timber-covered hills, "and you'll come out in another'n that'll take you down to the river below the falls. We might get there 'fore you, an' we'll tie up if'n we do, or you can just wait alongside an' we'll put in to take you back aboard. I want Ezra to stay aboard an' help with the sweeps."

Gabriel nodded his understanding and pushed the planks to the bank, and soon had the four horses unloaded. He had haltered the packhorses and saddled the black and Ezra's bay, and stood waiting for Persis. She soon appeared and bounced down the planks, anxious for the adventure of riding with Gabriel through the woods.

Gabriel was surprised to see she wore a split skirt, having never seen one before, and even more surprised when she straddled the saddle and smiled down at him as he stood agape. "What's the matter? Haven't you ever seen a woman on horseback before?"

"Uh, not like that, no."

"Oh, you mean with a split skirt?! I made it just for this purpose. I never could understand the whole side-saddle do'ins." She looked at him, "Well, are we going or not?"

Gabriel shook his head, swung aboard the black, picked up the leads of the two other horses, and started off, looking over his shoulder at the smiling Persis. She seemed to be quite adept at handling the bay.

With Rufus and Ezra manning the sweeps, Judson and Boxley standing ready to assist, Lucius at the rudder and Hamish on the gouger, they were ready to take on the rapids. Lucius had explained his tactic of staying as much in the middle of the current as possible while obviously avoiding any sawyers or rocks. He would holler out orders that they were to follow immediately. "These rapids drop about five feet or more in less'n a hundred yards. They're almighty noisy, so listen up, and look at me as often as you can." The men nodded and stepped to their long sweeps, keeping them out of the water until needed.

As the boat rounded the bend, there came in sight a long, narrow island, and the main current veered to the right. Lucius leaned into the rudder, keeping the boat well into the slow-moving current. To the right, the wide sandbank formed over millennia by the passage of the big river carrying silt from upstream showed good river bottom land. At the edge of the trees was the beginning of a cabin, but no one was in view. The timbered island slid along and slowly revealed the higher timbered bank on the left. Ezra went down on one knee and looked at the current, which seemed to be gaining in speed as it carried silt, wood, and debris from a rainfall upstream.

Lucius hollered for all to hear, "There's a strong eddy to the side yonder and a big rock beyond the falls. Hamish! You watch for that eddy and guide us past!" The big man lifted his hand in a wave, acknowledging his directions, but didn't turn back, keeping his eyes on the water before him. All the men stood, ready for the coming falls as the roar of the water alerted them to the nearness. They could see the churning white water and their bodies tensed with anticipation, hands gripping the long poles of the sweeps, feeling them bounce as the boat picked up speed.

As the prow of the boat hit the white water, the sound of the falls reverberated in the confines of the timbered banks, stifling the orders of the captain. Ezra and Rufus put their backs to the prow, focusing their attention on the captain and watching for his commands as he fought to steer the flat-bottomed broadhorn. The boat rocked from side to side and bounced front to back, water splashing over the prow and gunwales. Men staggered to keep their balance, gripping the poles. Suddenly the left sweep bounced and cracked, and the paddle end broke off, dropping Ezra flat on his back, still gripping the now-useless long pole. He stood, staggering to maintain his balance, and swung the end of the pole alongside, locking it in place, watching the captain.

Lucius was too busy with his own fight to concern himself with the broken oar. They would have to handle the boat without it. He barked orders to Rufus, "Pull! Hard! Keep us away from the eddy!" He nodded toward the big whirlpool that snatched at the broken paddle and began sucking it into the vortex. Hamish was fighting the gouger, pulling against the current that wrestled with the boat, trying to pull it to the whirlpool. Ezra ran to his side and lent his strength to the long sweep, and he saw Judson go to help Lucius.

The boat bucked and swayed, the creaking of the timbers muffled in the roar of the rapids. Time and again, one or another of the men lost their footing and fought to get upright and help with the big broadhorn. But the craft was not designed nor built for navigation, only as a barge for hauling, and it was more than a boxing match for the outweighed crew. The long oars bounced with the waves, dipping in and rising out of the water, fighting against the combined strength of the already tired men. Wide eyes watched as they neared the big eddy, but they fought on, pulling at the long sweeps, trying valiantly to wrest the boat away and win the tug of war with the malevolent maelstrom.

As suddenly as they had been tossed into the battle with the rapids, they were spat out the other end and floated blissfully, as if nothing had happened. Every man sat down in place, locking the oars in position and sucking air as if they had held their breath through the fight. They slowly looked to one another and frowns and scowls turned to grins. They struggled to their feet, awaiting the captain's orders.

"We'll put in yonder," declared Lucius, pointing to the lee side of the current and a small sandbank between some trees that marked a run from the hills. "Ezra, how 'bout you an' Judson here jump down an' get ready to tie us off!" Ezra grinned, waved at the captain, and started down the ladder, followed closely by Judson.

25 / Survivor

"It was under Chief Cornstalk that the Shawnee ceded the lands south of the Ohio River to the British. That was 'bout twenty years ago. But with the war, and Britain turning all the land over to the states, the Shawnee had kept fighting until the Battle of Fallen Timbers, when ol' General Wayne did his deed and defeated the combined confederacy. They're still negotiating, but the word is, all this will be open for new settlement. You know, like it is further east where your folks settled," explained Gabriel as the two rode the narrow trail through the timber, following the cut through the low hills.

"But do you think we'll ever have peace with the natives?" asked Persis, enjoying the lazy ride, listening to the creak of the saddle leather, the rattle of hooves on stone, and the calls of birds in the trees.

"Well, there are some who have become peaceful. Trouble is not just with the natives; much of the time it's with settlers who want their land and are willing to do just about anything to get the tribes gone. But from all I've learned, no matter how far we go into the wilderness, or what we call wilderness, there are more and more natives who were there long before any white man. So, I think it'll take more than some military man or politician crafting a treaty to make a lasting peace with the Indians. We have to learn to live together, to respect one another, and learn from one another. And from what little I know about the workings of the politicians, they can't even get along with each other, much less somebody from a different culture and history."

They broke from the thick timber to the shoulder of the hill overlooking the bottom land and the sandbank that stretched just about a half-mile to the edge of the river. To their right, or due north, they could see what was the river's long-ago route with the rise of the original bank, now brush and tree covered, that stood as a long ridge pointing to the far bend of the river. Before them stretched the grass and brush covered sandbank that Gabriel thought would one day be like so many other stretches of bottomland, covered with long rows of planted crops put in by some adventurous wannabe farmer. He looked to Persis, then back at the river, "I don't see the boat yet, but it might be moored by those trees yonder. We won't be able to see it until we get closer."

"I've enjoyed the ride so much. I'm not all that anxious to get back aboard!" declared a smiling Persis.

"I know what you mean. I'd much rather sit a saddle than stand on the deck of a boat, but it might be best if we kinda moseyed on down there. I saw some fresh tracks back there at the edge of that clearing. Might be Shawnee. This is their territory, after all."

"Where? How many? Did you see them, or just their tracks?" she asked frantically, looking around as if her head were on a swivel.

Gabriel chuckled, "Back there a ways, looked like maybe three or four, and all I saw was their tracks, so don't go gettin' all nervous on me. We'll just ride on down like nothing's wrong. We'll be fine, but how 'bout you leadin' the way just so's I can keep an eye on our backtrail?"

She gigged the bay to a trot and leaned into the gait, but Gabriel called out, "Easy! Just a walk will be fine."

She reined in the bay, turning to look at Gabriel with fear showing in her eyes as she hissed, "Hurry up! Let's go!"

The half-mile was covered in moments and Persis reined up at the bank of the river, stood in her stirrups, and searched up and down the wide water for the boat. She saw nothing until her eyes scanned the near bank. She leaned forward a little, shaded her eyes from the lowering sun and the glare off the water, then pointed, "What's that, there on the bank?!" she asked, looking to Gabriel. He moved the black alongside and looked where she pointed, scowled, and stepped to the ground. He walked to the bank and saw what looked like a piece of clothing or material awash on the strip of shore. He pushed aside the brush and walked closer, then, recognizing the form of a woman, he quickened his step and went to the figure. Kneeling down, he rolled her onto her back and was searching for any sign of life when a flutter of eyelids caught his attention. "Ma'am, ma'am, where are you hurt?"

A moan came from the woman, who had wet hair and mud covering much of her face, as she tried to move an arm and open her eyes. With wide eyes, she tried to move to escape the man who now held her and, gasping for air, she cried, "No! No!"

"Ma'am, I won't hurt you! We just found you!" pleaded Gabriel. Persis arrived at his side and knelt beside the woman.

"We're here to help you," she stated comfortingly. Upon seeing another woman, the waterlogged victim breathed easier, grasping at the hand of Persis. "Where are you hurt?" asked Persis.

"My neck, he tried to cut my throat, and then he stabbed me in the back before he threw me off the boat," she answered, struggling over every word and gasping for breath.

Persis examined first the woman's throat and it showed no injury, but after turning her on her side, there was blood on her back from at a cut in her bodice. Persis stuffed the cut with some material torn from the woman's petticoat, then rolled her to her back and helped her sit up.

"Your throat doesn't appear injured, but we'll do a better job on your back when our boat gets here," explained Persis.

"Oh, it must have been my tucker and mob that saved me," explained the woman.

Gabriel scowled, "Your what?"

Persis chuckled, "Her tucker is a ruffle around the collar or neck of the dress, and the mob is the cap that has lappets that protect the face and neck from the sun."

Gabriel slowly lifted his head, "Oh."

Persis turned to the woman, "My name is Persis, and this is Gabriel. May I have your name?"

"Of course, I am Charlotte Pelletier. We were returning to Gallipolis with some farm goods we purchased in Pittsburgh when we were set upon by some freebooters or pirates or whatever. Our boat had cleared the rapids, and they were lying in wait with their keelboat. They came upon us so quickly; the men didn't get off but one shot apiece." She dropped her head and sniffed, stifled a cry, and lifted her eyes to continue, "They killed everyone else, and tried to kill me. There were four men and two women, and they killed them all, then took everything and set fire to the boat. That's when they discovered us, Millicent and me. They shot her right off because she was a fighter and threw her over, then used a knife on me. I thought sure I was dead, but somehow, I made it to shore. I saw the boat going down just at the bend there," nodding downstream.

Gabriel stood tall, searching the water, and saw their boat nosing into the bank about forty yards upstream. He knew they could not see them for the thick brush along the bank, but it would be easy enough for them to make it that short distance. He turned to Persis, "The boat's putting in just up-stream a short way. I'll take the horses and come back in just a moment." He looked at Charlotte, "We'll be right back with something to carry you on, so don't try to walk." Both women nodded and watched as Gabriel turned away to gather the horses and fetch some help.

As Gabriel tethered the horses on the bank near the boat, Ezra stepped from the trees and, looking around, asked, "Uh, didn't you lose something?"

"Nope. Found something!"

Ezra looked around again, "I dunno. I'm pretty certain you left with a woman, but now you have none. So, that means you lost something."

"Nope. Found something, and you're gonna help me retrieve it." He stepped aboard the boat and fetched a wide board about eight feet long, then, with a nod of his head, he motioned for Ezra to come along. Stepping through the brush and down the bank, the two men laid the board beside the woman, and Gabriel, grinning, said, "Hop aboard your carriage, ma'am."

She smiled and held out her hand to Persis for some assistance, and lay back on the board as Gabriel introduced Ezra, "The other steed who shall power your carriage is known as Ezra. Ezra, this is Charlotte Pelletier."

"Ma'am, pleased to make your acquaintance, and contrary to what my friend implies, I am not a steed!"

The women giggled a bit and the levity seemed to cheer the woman up as she held tightly to the board while they negotiated the brush and the bank. Once safely aboard and in the cabin, Persis took over and made a pallet of blankets for the woman, talking all the while as they got acquainted with one another. True to the times and the territory, the woman proved to be very sturdy and strong-willed and insisted on helping where she could. While a weaker woman who had suffered the loss she had would be a blubbering, helpless waif, Charlotte proved to be quite resilient, and a friendship was quickly forming.

26 / Stratagem

"There was no warning! The men were exhausted from the rapids and were sitting down, away from their weapons. When the keelboat began to draw near, they ran for their rifles, but it was too late. Our men got off one shot before the freebooters caught hold with grappling hooks, and, oh! So unexpected! It was awful!" proclaimed Charlotte, dropping her face into her hands and sobbing. The two women were in the cabin and Persis had replaced the dressing on the stab wound in the woman's back, and they sat sipping cups of tea while Charlotte shared the memory.

"You're safe now. We have more men, more rifles, and a good crew. I'm sure no more harm will come to you," encouraged Persis, although a little uncertain herself. Gabriel had told her about the first attack on the boat and their successful defense, but that was mainly because Gabriel had been ashore and surprised the attackers. They might not be so lucky next time.

"I think we're only two days from Gallipolis," said Charlotte, more as a question than a statement.

"I believe so, yes, but we have to repair one of the long sweeps, or oars, for the boat before we can continue. The men are working on it now," explained Persis, sipping her tea. She looked to Charlotte, who squirmed a little in her seat, uncomfortable with the wound although it wasn't as serious as first thought. She had been protected by her stay, the stiff undergarment that would one day be called a corset. Persis asked, "I thought Gallipolis was a French settlement?"

"Oh, it is! Since the 'French 500' settled there, most of five years ago now. But we almost lost it when they found out our land titles were no good. We had purchased the land through the Scioto Company, but they didn't own it and had no right to sell it. But the last we heard; the President was going to make a grant of the land to our people."

"I don't understand. You don't sound French, but you are a part of the settlement?" asked Persis.

Charlotte smiled, "Well, you see, when the French came over and landed in Alexandria, they needed a guide to take them across country, and my brother, Charles, was chosen. But they also needed an interpreter, and since I am fluent in French, Charles recommended me. That was when I met Alexandre, who was an officer under Count Jean-Joseph de Barth, the leader of the group, who would later become my husband." She smiled at the memory and sat back and sipped at her tea, but tears filled her eyes as she thought about the skirmish and remembered her husband was dead.

Their tête-à-tête was interrupted by a clamor atop the cabin, and both ladies went to see what the ruckus was all about. The men had brought aboard a long tulip poplar tree that had been stripped of all its sprouts and was now being trimmed and shaped by Hamish and Gabriel. Lucius and Rufus and Judson were busy with the new blade for the oar, and Boxley had been relegated to cleanup duty. Ezra had taken the horses ashore for some fresh graze. Persis climbed the ladder to see and asked if anybody was ready for coffee, at which everyone stopped what they were doing and answered with a rousing "Yes!" causing Persis to quickly go to the stove and stoke up the fire.

"I just don't know what else we can do! We've got someone on watch all the time, our weapons are loaded and positioned, and everyone knows where they're supposed to be if an attack comes. What else can we do?" asked Lucius, looking around the circle of men.

"There's just no way of knowing what they'll do, or even which band of pirates it'll be!" added Hamish. "What we've seen before is they'll attack at night and try to sink the boat, or do like they did before—catch us comin' 'round a bend and try to jump us or shoot from the bank. That coulda been us when they hit that boat after the rapids." The others nodded their heads in agreement, looking into their coffee as their eyes glazed with their thinking and wondering.

"I remember my father always saying it's better to attack than defend, but not knowing where or who they are makes that more of a challenge. But one thing I know, though...I'd rather be ashore than cooped up in the cabin shootin' through a little hole!" offered Gabriel. The others chuckled and nodded in agreement.

As the men returned to their tasks, Lucius spoke to Gabriel, "If we do get jumped, you and Ezra are the ones I'll be dependin' on. None of these are fighting men, and you've already proven yourselves!"

Gabriel looked around, "I think all these men are capable fighting men. You and Hamish certainly proved that, and I think Rufus and Judson and his son will do all right. Even the women in the cabin; they've got backbone!"

They got on their way as Persis and Charlotte were finishing the noon meal and the men ate in shifts, making up a little for the lost time. Early on, everyone tensed up when they were overtaken by a keelboat, but it wasn't familiar and the crew seemed friendly enough, waving as they passed, but the men stayed close by their assigned stations in the event of a sneak attack, but it passed without incident.

By late afternoon, Lucius had negotiated the wide bend that swung west and pointed them south, and he chose to put in on the north shore, where a couple of cabins told of new settlers on the long strip of bottom land. As they tied the boat off, Lucius pulled out his bugle and sounded it loud and clear, doubling his call as he faced the south shore as well. He looked at the men, "We might even get a few Shawnee, we've traded with 'em before, but that was before these new settlers built their cabins here. We might have to put 'er over to the other shore yonder if'n we don't get any tradin' here'bouts."

But they were not to be disappointed. Four couples came to the bank, one with a two-wheel cart loaded with pelts and vegetables for trading. "Howdy!" declared a whiskery grey-haired man with high-water britches held up by galluses that showed his well-worn boots. His linen shirt had seen much use and many washings, and refused to stay tucked into his britches, even with the aid of the galluses. His wide grin parted the whiskers, displaying tobacco-stained teeth, what few there were, and mischief danced in his eyes. His woman was in a long woolen dress and wore a facial expression almost as long. Tight-lipped and grey-haired, she never spoke a word, but often grunted at her husband's remarks. The other three couples reflected similar visages, and Gabriel thought this must be an extended family, which he soon found to be an accurate assumption.

When all was said and done, they swapped a barrel of whiskey, one of the remaining three stoves, the rest of the pigs, and half the remaining chickens for a stack of pelts that included a panther, two badgers, one skunk, eight deer, two bears, and four bushels of fresh vegetables including three kinds of squash, carrots, lettuce, cabbage, beans, and okra. Persis and Charlotte were especially pleased by the variety of vegetables, with Charlotte saying, "Whatever you folks don't want, I'm sure my people at Gallipolis will trade for them!"

Several folks were waiting on the south shore, and once their trade was complete with the first group, they moved south and started all over. But by suppertime, trading was done, the boat was safely moored, and the men were properly hungry.

Gabriel had moved onshore with the horses, staking them out in a cutaway in the tree line well-covered by a hedgerow of rocks and chokecherry and buttonbush. He put his saddle against a big sugar maple and rolled out his blankets. The tree stood on a slight rise, and when standing, he could see over the brush across the sandbank to the boat. With a three-quarter moon, he would be able to see most of the area around the mooring.

The sun had bounced its last shards of color off the placid river, and Gabriel had enjoyed the display of the Creator's majesty before making a check on each of the horses. They were contentedly enjoying the tall grass and lifted their heads as he neared, Ebony giving a low nicker at his approach. He stepped close and the big black tucked his nose under Gabriel's arm to receive his stroking and petting, a custom between the two best friends. "Good boy. Ya miss me, didja?" He stroked the horse's neck and ran his fingers through the mane of the big black, when Ebony lifted his head, ears pricked, and looked toward the river. Gabriel turned to see Persis coming toward them, the grass coming up to her waist and making it appear as if she were swimming through the greenery, now muted by the lowering light of dusk.

She saw she was watched and waved, calling, "Thought you might like some coffee before you turn in!" lifting a pot and cup high. He waved back and started to his perch under the maple, pushing a flat rock near for either Persis or the coffee pot, her choice.

As they were seated on his blankets, the pot on the stone, Persis asked, "You don't think the keelboat that passed us was pirates, do you?"

"Oh, probably not. There are more honest boatmen than pirates, and we can't go thinking just that because it's a keelboat, it means they're pirates. They appeared friendly enough and no one looked familiar, so probably not," answered Gabriel.

They visited for a short while, but as dusk dropped its mantle of darkness to kiss the treetops and stretch the shadows of night, Gabriel said, "I better walk you back to the boat. You might lose your way!"

"Ha! I love the night, and I can find my way by the stars!" she declared, smiling. "But, since you're a proper gentleman, I will let you escort the lady back." As they walked, pushing through the deep grass, they watched as the first stars lit their lanterns of silver and the constellations began to paint their pictures across the heavens. Persis pointed, "See! There's Ursa Major!" pointing to the constellation that some were calling the Big Dipper.

Gabriel smiled and pointed, "And there, see the three stars in a row? That's Orion, the mighty hunter!"

They laughed with one another, enjoying the brief respite from the work and worry of the day, but grew quiet as they neared the boat. Everyone had turned in, knowing the morrow would call for an early start, but Ezra quietly stood in the shadows, watching and listening as the waves beat their rhythm on the hull. Gabriel gave Persis a hand but heard a hiss from the shadow and froze in place, eyes on Ezra. He pushed Persis against the cabin and stealthily started toward Ezra, but he had gone to the gunwale and leaned slightly over, looking at the water. Gabriel saw his friend had his warclub in hand, held shoulder-high.

"I don't take kindly to people sneakin' up on our boat in the night!" He spoke in a calm, normal tone, but slowly lifted the warclub. Suddenly he swung it down and Gabriel heard a *thunk* that made him think of a splitting melon, followed by a choking cry and a panicked splash of water. A scrape of some-thing sharp on the wood followed, then the rhythmic splashes of the waves returned and Ezra leaned over, dunking his war-club's blade in the water, then stood and turned to Gabriel.

"Don't know if there's more, but we better have a look-see."

Gabriel nodded, and the two started in opposite directions to search the water for more two-legged rats. Ezra went to the prow and Gabriel to the stern, out of sight of Persis as she stood frozen in the shadow. Suddenly a shot came from the rear of the boat, then another, then silence. The others atop the cabin came quickly awake and searched the darkness for the cause of the shot. Lucius was the first to shout, "It's Gabriel, here at the stern!"

Gabriel made his way to the front of the boat where the others had gathered, and Ezra and Persis appeared. When they looked to Gabriel, he nodded to Ezra for him to explain. "I think they were tryin' that trick you told us about, Captain. I got one here at the side of the boat, and when he tried to throw a knife, I discouraged him. Then we split up, and I'm guessin' Gabriel found 'nother'n. Right?"

Gabriel chuckled, "Ummhumm. I just winged him on the first shot, but the second one sank him. Took a moment to turn it over for the second barrel. Glad I had it since I needed that second shot!"

"Then we need to check below for any leaks. They usually try to pull out the caulking or drill holes in the wood. If we get on it now, we can get 'er fixed and still get a good night's sleep." The men set to work, but no leaks were found. "Reckon you two caught 'em 'fore they could do any damage, but they won't stop at that. We'll have to be doubly watchful!" declared Lucius. All the men nodded and turned away to go to their blankets. Persis surprised Gabriel with a hug to send him back to his place with the horses, and he smiled all the way.

27 / Pirates

The dim grey of early morning light made a silhouette of Gabriel as he led the horses to the broadhorn. Lucius had been up for a spell, waiting for him, and lifted a hand in a wave as he came through the dogwood, pushing aside the branches clustered with the flat-topped white blossoms. Gabriel started to give a "mornin'" shout but was stayed by a motion to silence from the captain. As he drew near, Lucius leaned over the gunwale and spoke softly, "I was thinkin' after that set-to last night, I don't think the pirates are too far away. We're nigh unto twenty miles from Gallipolis, and ain't much 'tween here and there." He stood upright, pointing downstream, "Just 'round that bend, the east bank rises up two to three hundred feet, steep-sided but thick timber. That tall timber goes down to the waterline, and it would be a prime hidin' spot for pirates. 'Course, there's no way to know for sure, but if'n it were me, I could hide a boat in those trees purty easy." He squatted down next to the gunwale, looking sternly at Gabriel, "Now, you saved our bacon last time 'cuz you was in the trees, an' it'd sure make me feel better if'n I knowed you was in amongst 'em again."

Persis had heard the captain speaking and peered around the corner of the cabin to see Gabriel nearing the boat. She smiled, turned away, and fetched a steaming cup of coffee, returning with a smile that Gabriel thought was brighter than the morning light.

He smiled at her and reached for the offered cup, "Thank you, m'lady!" he declared. "I don't think I'll be around for breakfast, but if you've got a couple of those biscuits, I'd admire to have them if you don't mind."

"They're almost done, so I will fetch you some," she answered, smiling coyly.

Gabriel turned back to the captain, "I'd like Ezra to come with me if you can spare him."

"Of course. I'll have Hamish and Rufus atop with me, and Judson and his son can handle things in the cabin. The women can reload as necessary, or even use a rifle if they're of a mind to."

"Good. I think their tactic last time was to push the boat into the preferred bank by firing on you from the far shore, thinkin' you'd retreat to the near shore where the rest of 'em lay in wait. They might try that again."

"There's a lot of different tactics they use, like they did with Charlotte's boat. Used a ruse to get near, then opened fire on 'em. We'll just have to be wary of any trick," suggested the captain.

Ezra had pushed the planks back to the bank, thinking Gabriel was loading all the horses, but when he looked at his friend, he was told of the plan. They loaded the packhorses on the boat, and Ezra brought his saddle and gear down to ready himself for the day's ride. By the time he tightened the girth, Persis had returned with Gabriel's biscuits, and seeing Ezra, she said, "So, I suppose I need to bring a few more biscuits? And would you like something additional for later?"

Gabriel chuckled, "No, just the biscuits will be fine," then bit into one that was still quite warm and slathered with butter and honey traded from the farmers. As Persis started back to the cabin, Gabriel called, "Uh, maybe a few more biscuits?" She smiled and turned away to her morning's mission.

* * * * *

"Those two imbeciles you sent last night apparently didn't do the job!" sneered Ian, looking at the captain of the keelboat, Jacob Langdon.

"They was good men. Never failed me afore, but I reckon sumpin' happened to 'em."

"That boat should be heavy with water and stuck in the shallows at the shore, but I'd lay odds they're getting underway!" growled Ian Soames.

Shorty had come forward when he heard the men talking. He rubbed the sleep from his eyes, stretched, and caught a glare from Soames. "I'm guessin' by that look and your arguin' that the first part of your plan didn't work out, am I right?"

"You're right! This, this," motioning to the bulbous captain, who stood glaring and hitching up his britches that always seemed to retreat from his midriff of fat, "this poor excuse for a captain sent a couple imbeciles on a job for a man. They haven't returned!" Soames turned away to lean on the gunwale, looking upstream at the river, seeing the dim light of morning beginning to bounce crooked beams on the waves.

Shorty looked from the cowering captain to the angry Soames, then looked at the river and the far bank and thought for a moment. He leaned out over the water, looking both upstream and down, then straightened up and looked at Soames. "Give me a couple your men, and me and mine'll take 'em with us to the far bank. We'll come from there and flag 'em down like we want to trade, then we'll hit 'em hard and fast. Then you and your men can join in the fun, and we'll divvy up later!" He grinned broadly as if he had just solved everyone's problems and leaned back against the rail to wait for an answer from Soames.

Soames gave him a sidelong glance, then looked at the river again. He lifted his eyes to the far shore and then behind him and up and downstream. He had tried the friendly approach with traders before and it seldom worked, especially from a flimsy canoe where there was no cover. And with those aboard this boat, if they were the same ones they had tangled with before, anyone in the canoes would be an easy target. As he considered everything, he let a slow grin paint his face. He thought this might be an easy way to eliminate Shorty's crew and not have to divvy up the reward. All that gave him pause was that he didn't know where or who to go to for the reward, but maybe that could be resolved another way.

He looked at the little man, then lifted his eyes and hand to point downstream, "There is a better place for that kind of attack down there where the sandbank meets the timber. That'll give you cover until the boat nears. We'll move down on this side, there." He pointed to a place where the bank had caved away, dropping several trees into the water with their roots still in the bank. The fallen timber was a natural catch-all for any driftwood or debris and made a dam-like barrier and cover for the keelboat.

The three men talked a little more about their plan of attack until Shorty interrupted, "If we're doin' it, I want somethin' to eat first! Your men on the bank gotta a fire goin'? They cookin' some breakfast?"

Soames stared at the man and fought to control his irritation and anger, then turned toward the bank, "Looks like it! Let's get it over with so we can get to our places!"

Shorty grinned, "That suits me just fine!" He stepped to the rail and swung over, caught the ladder with his toes, and quickly stepped to the shore.

Soames hung back and spoke to Langdon, his captain, "I want the best men on the boat. Put ten or twelve on this shore, and send two with them," nodding his head toward Shorty. "It was just our luck that we ran into Indians the last time, but that won't happen again. After those on the broadhorn shoot the canoes full of holes, we'll take the boat from this side, and we'll also be free of that bunch!"

The captain grinned at Soames, "I like your thinkin' boss! Anybody you don't like you wanna send in the canoes?"

"You pick 'em, I don't care."

Shorty had trotted off toward the camp and clapped his hands as he neared the fire as he called out, "Today's the day! We're doin' it, boys!" and was glad to see the smiles on his three crewmen. They stood as he neared, "Let's get some breakfast, then we'll get set!" he ordered.

* * * * *

As they entered the trees, they split up. With Gabriel taking the uphill side and Ezra the downhill, they needed to find a game trail to get them through the thick timber. With so much downed timber, limbs, and undergrowth, it would be impossible to traverse the side slope without sounding like a herd of buffalo crashing through the timber. Gabriel was the first to give the familiar call of the red-tailed hawk. Ezra answered with the long descending scream-whistle sound, and Gabriel waited for him to come close. When he neared, Gabriel pointed to the dim trail that led around the knob of the hill and appeared to traverse the slope. With Gabriel in the lead, the men gave the horses their heads and let them walk on the leaf-covered trail. With the morning dew still heavy in the woods, the men were often seen ducking their heads into their collars as the moisture dripped from overhanging branches, seeking a way to trail the water down their backs.

Suddenly, Gabriel lifted his hand and reined up. He

looked back to Ezra, pointed to his own nose, and made the sign with his fingers the two used to indicate smoke. Ezra frowned, stood in his stirrups, and lifted his head, sniffing for the smoke. Turning slightly downhill, he nodded, then pointed. Gabriel nodded in agreement and the men slipped from their saddles, tethered their horses, and with rifles in hand, started through the trees.

This was a forest that had probably never seen a white man before. Indians maybe, but mostly wild game. They stealthily picked their way, choosing each step carefully, always keeping several trees in a direct line between them and the direction from which they believed the smoke had emanated. The leaf-littered woods often concealed dead branches, and one misstep could betray their presence. Ezra was slightly below Gabriel, and he suddenly stopped, pointing to the ground. That same instant, Gabriel heard a slithering sound in the leaves, and his eyes grew wide as he stood tiptoed, searching the leaves. A fat, coiled snake about three feet long stared at Gabriel. It rattled its stubby rattles as Gabriel tried to lean away, but every move was followed by the snake, feinting several strikes. Gabriel felt his heart wanting to beat its way out of his chest, his eyes stretched wide, and sweat ran from his forehead and armpits. He gripped the rifle stock tightly, wanting to strike out at the snake before the rattler could strike him.

The long barrel of Ezra's flintlock slowly reached out and pushed at the snake, making it strike at the barrel, but failing, the snake turned and slithered off through the leaves. Gabriel watched the movement of the damp floor of the forest that showed the snake's escape. He let his breath go, realizing he had held it all this time, and looked at Ezra. Both men knew the fear Gabriel had always had for snakes. Breathing deeply in relief, he nodded to his friend and shook his head as they resumed their search for the source of the smoke.

They had scarcely gone another ten yards when they were stopped by the sounds of wood on wood and muffled voices. They each dropped to one knee, looking under the low branches of the hardwoods, and listened. It was the sound of men breaking camp and loading their boat. Gabriel looked to Ezra, and with signs, indicated he would go to the left and try to see more as Ezra went the opposite way. With a nod to one another, the men started off slowly and stealthily. Gabriel came near the camp but stayed well back in the trees, then dropped to his belly to crawl closer. He saw the men loading their gear aboard the keelboat but couldn't make out what was being said, and he dared not go nearer. Once all were aboard, the lines were cast aboard, and the keelboat nosed into the current. He watched as it started downstream and drifted out of sight.

He stood and walked back up the hillside, meeting Ezra as they neared the horses. "I didn't hear or see anything that made me think they were getting ready to attack, did you?"

Ezra scowled, "Didn't you see the canoes?"

Gabriel stopped and stared at his friend, "Canoes?"

"Yeah, two canoes, three men in each, all with rifles. They moved out just before the keelboat and headed across the river. Looked to me like they were settin' a trap!"

Without another word, they trotted to the horses and swung aboard, knowing they had to find where the keelboat would lie in wait and where the shooters would be positioned if they were to have any hope of saving their friends aboard the flatboat.

28 / Encounter

They were about a hundred and fifty feet above the level of the river, but even by line-of-sight, they were a quarter-mile from the water's edge. They stayed to the game trail that often forked with a branch headed downhill, the path taken by thirsty game to get to the water, but they chose the high ground. Whenever the trees thinned, they would search the river for the keelboat, occasionally getting a glimpse as it allowed the current to carry it down, giving little effort to anything but the tiller. After a little over a mile, the trees crowded in among them, and Ezra had to shinny up a tall tulip poplar to see the river. After a few tries, climbing higher, leaning out on a branch, squirming around, and looking every bit the squirrel, he spotted the boat a little further downstream. He slid down, dropped to the ground, and looked to Gabriel, "Looks like they might be puttin' in. There's a narrow ridge that follows the river, then a bigger hill kinda pushes out into the channel. I think they're putting in behind that hill."

"Then let's get a move on an' see if we can get a handle on what they're up to!" declared Gabriel, handing the reins of the bay to Ezra. The trail they followed traced the contour of the land, climbing the side slopes of the hills and dropping into the cuts that held streambeds or thick brush. Gabriel looked around at the variety of hardwood trees, maples, oaks, and sycamore and knew at any other time, he would enjoy the handiwork of the Creator. With the many calls of songbirds, warblers and their sweet-sweet-sweeter than sweet notes, the chattering of the woodpecker, and the tweedle-dee of the blue jay, along with the musty smells of decaying leaves blending with the cool breeze of the morning, it would be an enjoyable ride, but today was different. Today they were facing a deadly threat from those who would steal and kill. As his thoughts turned to the impending battle, the familiar tenseness took hold and he gritted his teeth, nostrils flaring, then flexed his shoulder muscles, dark eyes glaring into the thick tree cover.

They dropped into a cut between the hills, and Gabriel recognized the narrow creek as the one Lucius had spoken of when he'd described the country to Gabriel. "I think this is the one Lucius called Ice Creek." Ezra nodded, then pointed to the hogback ridge that paralleled the river and the turtle hump of a hill beyond. He gigged his horse forward to take the lead, having seen this from his lofty perch in the trees. The horses moved as silently as possible, picking their steps on the ancient trail now littered with dew-covered leaves. Where they were bound, there was no game trail, and Ezra's horse wound in and out among the trees, moving with the pressure given by his rider's knees. In a short while, he led them around the knob of the hill, and a break in the trees gave them an overview of the river below.

If they could see, they could be seen, so they moved the horses into the trees and stepped down to return to the break. Each dropped to one knee, lowering their profile and visibility but still craning to see below. "There, you can see the stern of the keelboat!" declared Ezra, pointing.

"Yeah. Now where are the shooters gonna be?" asked Gabriel, moving from side to side, trying to get a glimpse through the thick woods.

Ezra stood, leaned to the side, and searched below, "There! Looks like they're lining out on the bank like they did before."

"I see 'em. Any idea how many?" asked Gabriel, still scanning the trees. With no response from Ezra, he lifted his eyes to the far bank, "And there's the canoes!" pointing with his chin. Across the river, which was about four hundred yards wide, the two birchbark canoes sat empty, rocking in the water. Standing behind them was a group of men, six by Ezra's count from when he saw the canoes leave the keelboat. They surveyed the area below, where the lower quarter of the hill spread in a shoulder sparsely covered with brush, then dropped into the river. The boat was just at the end of the shoulder, and the tree cover upstream of their location would afford the best cover for a surprise attack. Once the keelboat was sighted, all possibility of surprise for the attackers would be gone, but it was well-concealed behind the overhanging trees that dipped with their low branches dragging in the water.

Killing does not come naturally to any man. Some become conditioned to it after encounters in war or other conflicts, while others can never bring themselves to deal in death under any circumstances. In those cases, there are only two means of recourse; someone else has to do the defending and killing, or they must resign themselves to dying. Those who stand and protect others are the ones who build great nations and lay the foundations for good and moral people to build upon.

Neither Gabriel nor Ezra savored the task before them, but others were depending on them to make the way safe, and that would require dealing to others what they were eager to rain down upon innocents solely for one reason: money. There are always those who are willing to earn what they get and others who would rather take from those who work, being too lazy or immoral to honestly build their own lives.

Taking a deep breath of resolve, the two friends stood and went to the horses for their weapons. Gabriel took one of the saddle pistols, checked the loads, and stuffed it in his belt beside the Bailes turnover pistol. He slipped the second saddle pistol from its holster and handed it to Ezra. He quietly accepted the bigger pistol and slipped it into his britches next to his own. While Gabriel would have his Mongol bow and arrows, two double-barreled pistols, and his Ferguson rifle, Ezra had his Lancaster-style long rifle, built by the well-respected crafts- man Jacob Dickert, the double-barreled pistol from Gabriel, his own pistol, and his war-club. Both men also carried a knife and a tomahawk and were skilled at throwing and using them.

They moved from the edge of the slight clearing where the

horses were already contentedly enjoying the grass and moving into the trees, staying five to ten yards apart. They knew that when moving close together, the sound was magnified and more easily located. They traveled as quickly as possible, maintaining their stealth but needing to get to their quarry before the battle started. It was their job to equalize the odds.

* * * * *

Persis chose to take on the reloading of rifles atop the cabin. Her concern was for her brother, Rufus, and the two always worked well together, often anticipating the other's actions and reactions. Charlotte would tend to the same duties in the cabin, helping Judson and his son, Boxley. But both women were experienced with rifles and were willing to give a hand when needed. Atop the cabin, the new addition of the stacked log breastworks gave cover, as long as they kept their heads down, and within the cabin, the heavy slotted shutters protected the shooters. Every shooting position held at least one rifle, with a powder horn and possibles pouch with balls and patches nearby.

Lucius had given Gabriel and Ezra close to two hours' lead time, believing the extra time would also give the pirates concern, and maybe make them anxious enough to prematurely show their hand. Finally, they pushed away from the bank, and with the side sweeps pulling, the boat was soon midstream and moving with the current. Rufus and Hamish lifted the sweeps from the water, laying them alongside the cabin's breastworks, and turned a watchful eye on the river. Lucius was at the tiller, ever searching the tree line on both banks for any sign of the pirates. The broadhorn took the wide bend as the river slowly and pointed to the southwest. Wide sandbanks and bottom land with sparse brush and grass pushed the hills back from the right bank, while on the left, timber-covered hills crowded the steep bank, rising like prehistoric monsters sleeping side by side, muzzles at the water. The lazy river moved on a straight southwesterly course for about two and a half miles before bending to the south. It was at that dogleg that Lucius had told Gabriel would be a prime location for an attack. He shook his head at the thought, breathed deep, and took a firm stance to ready himself for whatever would come.

Lucius watched as Hamish and Rufus made another check of each rifle. With three rifles per side and one beside Lucius, they were as prepared as possible. Persis sat toward the back of the cabin watching her brother, her lips moving in silent prayer. Lucius knew that within the cabin, the same thing was happening; rifles were being checked and Charlotte probably praying. That was alright with him. He believed in prayer and had already spent a little time doing that very thing. But now, he watched the river.

The surface of the water was placid, and the murky water secreted the depths from discovery. Occasionally, some driftwood could be seen, and one tree trunk held an otter that hitched a ride while he dozed. Overhead, a red-tailed hawk circled, looking for his dinner, and the rattle of a woodpecker could be heard as he drilled his holes in the hardwood. It was a peaceful scene and one that could be enjoyed, except for the danger that lurked silently below.

Lucius first scanned the thicker trees to his left, then searched the flats and brush to his right. Just beyond the downstream edge of the bottomland, trees overhung the river's edge, and movement caught his eye. Then the prows of two birchbark canoes slid from under the overhanging trees, and the figures of six men showed. Lucius called out, "Here they come!"

Hamish looked at the canoes as the flatboat and birchbarks neared. One of the men in the canoes waved his paddle in the air and shouted, "We wanna trade! Got some pelts!" Hamish looked to Lucius, "What if they're not pirates? They say they wanna trade. We can't shoot innocent settlers!"

29 / Fight

Gabriel and Ezra had often spent time in the woods, learning to move as silently as the soft breeze of early morning, and now that practice was proving its worth. A squirrel chattered its displeasure, and a red-bellied woodpecker sounded its mimicry of the echoing reverberations of its own work. Their moccasins gave them the feel of each obstacle and they stepped lightly, ever vigilant of the men below them. Gabriel was the first to see a man, and with a sudden hand signal, alerted Ezra. They crouched within reach of one another, searching the line of dogwood for more shooters. The attackers held their positions well, seldom moving, but each move revealed a target for the two friends. Ezra pointed to the river, where they saw the canoes beginning to move from their cover. Now was the time, and as agreed, they separated, each moving to opposite ends of the line of attackers to begin their work.

Trusting those aboard the flatboat with their own tasks, Gabriel nocked an arrow, picking his first target and the subsequent two. Once settled where he could move through the trees and still have a firing lane with each stop, he let fly the first arrow. Not waiting to see it strike, he moved quickly to his second position, hearing his arrow find its mark, and a muted grunt from the man told him one target was down. As he found his second position, he thought how foolish it was of the attackers to use a tactic that had failed them before, but men are creatures of habit, seldom changing their ways unless it is forced upon them.

Ezra had marked his targets, but preferring close-in work, he started with the man at the end. He quietly stepped behind him and reached around to grab his chin and mouth with his left hand, his right hand held his razor-sharp knife, and with one swift move, he slit the man's throat from ear to ear. His victim kicked out, but not strongly enough to sound a warning. Ezra slowly let the man's body slide to the ground and started for the next one. The second man was restless and started to turn just as Ezra stepped from the brush. He flipped his knife to catch it by the tip and threw it with such force that it buried itself to the hilt in the man's throat, causing him to rise to his feet and, choking on his own blood, fall on his face. Ezra, in a crouch, moved closer, pushed the man to his back, and jerked out his knife, wiping it on the man's shirtfront.

His third target was nestled in some thick brush with no easy access, but Ezra grinned and pulled his long-handled war-club from the sling at his back, leaving his flintlock untouched. He dropped to a crouch and, using the same brush as his cover, moved closer. When he came to the edge of the brush, he pushed aside a handful of the thicket, saw the back of the man waiting with his rifle before him, anticipating a shot at the flatboat, and grinned. He slowly rose to his full height, lifted the warclub overhead, and with practiced precision, threw the club cartwheeling over the brush to bury the broad axehead at the base of the man's neck, severing his spinal cord and driving him head-first into his covering brush.

Gabriel had scored on two targets, and no alarm had been given as he moved to his third position. He stood beside a towering tulip poplar, nocking his arrow. He brought the bow to full draw and loosed the missile of death on its path, but he was suddenly knocked to the ground, and a searing pain stabbed his hip as he fell. Startled, he caught himself, still holding onto his bow, and rolled to the trunk of the tree, searching for his assailant. He looked beneath the branches of the nearby trees, then saw what had struck him. He gave a quick closer look, then, surprised at seeing the dart, searched higher. There, high in that sycamore, a man was struggling with his feet in the limbs. Next to the riser, he sought to pull the crossbow to full draw, ready to fire another bolt. But he would not get the chance, since Gabriel had automatically nocked another arrow while he was searching the trees. He quickly lifted the bow and let fly another arrow that wedged itself between the man's elbow and thigh, penetrating the lower gut and pinning the man to the tree trunk. With a gasp and a gurgle of blood, the man's head fell forward and he let go of the crossbow, letting it clatter to the ground. Gabriel quickly vacated his position, dropping to his belly behind a thick oak and bringing his Ferguson rifle from its sling at his back.

*   *   *   *   *

After Lucius' shouted alarm, everyone watched the approach of the canoes, breathlessly waiting for anyone to take action. In the cabin, Charlotte was peering through one of the firing slits, and her eyes grew wide as she whispered, "He's one of them!" Then, realizing what she discovered, she shouted, "They're pirates! That man is one of those who attacked our boat!"

At her first alarm, Judson took aim on the man in the front of the nearest canoe and touched off his round. The man rose slightly, grabbing at his chest, and fell over the gunwale of the canoe, rocking the others as they grabbed at their rifles. At the first shot, Boxley also fired, as did those atop the cabin, and suddenly the river erupted with rifle fire. Rufus aimed for the man in the prow of the second canoe, and red blossomed on the man's throat as he dropped the paddle and grabbed at his wound, falling forward and rolling to the side to fall into the water.

Hamish hesitated, trying to choose a target, then fired at the first canoe, his ball striking the water beside the boat. He scrambled for another rifle, was handed one by Persis, and turned to take aim again. Rufus, lying prone behind a notch in the breastwork, squeezed off a shot and saw another man grab at his shoulder, dropping his rifle into the river. He grinned and handed his rifle to his sister to reload as he looked at the others in the canoes, now bringing their rifles to bear on the flatboat. As Persis struggled to reload without making a target of herself, she focused on driving the ramrod home and heard Rufus grunt and let a slow groan escape. She looked up to see her brother roll to his side, eyes staring at the sky, with a bullet hole in the center of his forehead. Persis screamed, dropped the rifle, and crawled to her brother's side, pulling him to her as she touched his face. Tears filled her eyes, and she felt herself sob as she clawed at his jacket, trying to will life back into him.

Lucius had unconsciously steered the boat farther away from the canoes, but seeing Rufus hit, he released the tiller and dropped to his knees to snatch up a rifle and fire at those who were left in the canoes. He took a steady aim at the man in the middle of the first boat, squeezed off his shot and through the smoke belched from the rifle, he saw the man fall backward into the bottom of the boat. Two men remained, one in each boat, and Lucius crabbed his way to another rifle, sat up, and took aim. He squeezed off another shot and saw his target roll from the boat into the water, but he wasn't sure how bad the man was hit.

Below, Judson lined up his sights on the last man, now trying to backpaddle to get away, but Judson's shot was true and the bullet bored its way into the man's chest, making him fall to the side and overturn the canoe. Then the river was silent and the canoes, one upright, the other bottom-up, drifted with the current, companions to the big flatboat.

But peace and quiet were not to be; gunfire erupted from the shore, and everyone turned their attention to the thick trees and the puffs of smoke that lanced their way from the greenery.

* * * * *

When the gunfire erupted on the boat, those onshore knew there was no longer a need for the pretense of silence, but with the flatboat still in midstream, a shot from the shore would be at least two hundred and fifty yards, and accuracy would be difficult at best. But not so with Gabriel and Ezra and their targets. With the attention of the would-be assailants focused on the flatboat and the canoes, Gabriel and Ezra made their way down the line, picking their targets. Gabriel was the first to mark his next one. Again choosing his Mongol bow, he took the next one in line and nocked another arrow, but was startled when a bullet whipped past his head, making him drop to the brush. He swung his Ferguson from its sling, checked the load, and moved in a low crouch, rifle at his chest. The rustle of brush gave him only an instant's warning, and he brought the muzzle of the rifle around as he faced the charge of a man with a pistol in one hand and a tomahawk in the other, screaming as he lunged. All Gabriel could do was lift the rifle to stop the hawk, but the man discharged the pistol held low, and Gabriel felt the heat and impact of the bullet in the same hip that had caught the crossbow quarrel.

He stumbled to the side, using the rifle as a club to

knock the man to his knees, but he was quick to rise, toma-hawk still in his hand. Gabriel dropped his rifle as he grabbed for his pistol and, drawing it, he brought it to full cock, put his finger on the forward trigger, and fired. The cloud of powder smoke blackened the man's middle, but the bullet tore a hole that bled across the black, forming a crude blossom of death as the man fell backward, looking down at his belly. He looked up at Gabriel, "You kilt me!" he growled as his legs gave out and he crumpled to fall on his face.

As he searched the brush for another attacker, Gabriel twisted the over-under barrel of the pistol to bring the loaded barrel to the top, jammed it back in his belt, and picked up the Ferguson. He looked down at his hip, buckskins blackened with the pistol shot from the freebooter, and winced as he saw the wound, then shook his head, knowing the blast from the pistol had cauterized the wound from the crossbow bolt. He also knew the bullet had done some damage. He winced again as he put his weight on that leg, but there was more to do. This bunch of shooters were not in a line like the last bunch; these were scattered in the thick brush and were harder to find.

A shot came from his right and it sounded like the roar of the big saddle pistol and Gabriel grinned, believing Ezra had scored a hit against the pirate crew, but he couldn't concern himself with that; there were more nearby. He looked at the water and saw the flatboat nearer the shore than expected and suddenly a barrage of rifle fire came from below him, each cloud of smoke marking the position of a shooter. Gabriel marked them as best he could and started after the nearest.

In the excitement, the shooters on shore all cut loose at the same time, making it necessary for each to reload before doing any more damage. That brief delay gave those aboard the flatboat a few moments to use the side sweeps and move away from the shore and more into the current. With the attention of the shooters focused on reloading, Gabriel quickly made his way to the nearest man and ended his efforts with a swift blow of the tomahawk. When the man dropped to the ground, he dropped his rifle and kicked at the brush, alerting the nearest shooter.

Gabriel dropped to one knee behind a thick button brush just as a bullet crashed through the branches near his head. He unconsciously ducked his head into his neck, chuckling at his own turtle-like reaction when he heard Ezra say, "Comin' in, don't shoot!" The brush parted as a grinning Ezra looked at his friend, "Glad to see they ain't kilt you yet!"

"Likewise," replied Gabriel. "But we need to keep 'em from shootin' at the boat! There's at least four more down in the brush thataway," he said, pointing with his chin. "I'll go thisaway, then stand up and shoot at 'em while you go thata-way and pick 'em off as they try to get me!"

"All right give me a minute," answered Ezra as he crabbed back through the brush, moving down the slope toward the remaining shooters. Gabriel moved to the side, careful not to move any brush that would give away his location, then, satisfied with his position, he eared the hammer back on the Ferguson and slowly stood, his finger on the forward trigger.

He had marked the position of the shooters, but this was a different angle, so he shouted, "Hey!" to see any movement. One man nearby twisted at the shout, wanting to see who was coming; his movement was a giveaway, and Gabriel readied his shot as the man lifted his head above the top of the brush. The bullet bored into his brain, knocking him into eternity and the dogwood. Another shooter, thinking Gabriel's rifle was now empty and he'd have to reload, stood and brought his rifle around, but before he could fire, Ezra's rifle spoke and sent a message of deliverance.

The other shooters, two or three of them, scattered through the brush, staying low and out of sight as they scrambled back to the keelboat. Without another clear shot, Gabriel and Ezra let them go and started for the shore to signal their flatboat. They crashed through the brush, anxious to bring in their boat before they reached the lying-in-wait keelboat, and Ezra jumped and waved, catching the attention of Lucius, who leaned into the rudder and pointed the boat to shore.

30 / Stolen

Kavanagh was in the back of the canoe and watched as the others took lead. He looked at the flatboat, saw the glint of light from the barrel of a rifle atop the cabin, and figured the safest place would be in the water. He leaned over just as a bullet whistled past his head, and he dove into the water on the far side of the canoe, but the birchbark tipped with him and turned over, yet still shielding him from the flatboat.

Kavanagh was an excellent swimmer. He had been pressed into service in the British Navy and jumped ship from a frigate when the ships were trapped inside the Chesapeake Bay by the French Admiral de Grasse. He had swum to shore, a distance of well over a mile. After a quick look at the activity on the flatboat, he dove deep and swam toward the slow-moving craft. He kicked and pulled at the water, slowly letting his wind escape, but soon had to surface for air. He slowly put just his face above the surface, then turned to the side for a quick look at the broadhorn. He grinned as he dove under again, and with a few more kicks, he surfaced at the stern of the boat, out of sight below the gunwale. He breathed heavily, catching his wind and readying himself for whatever was to come next.

Once he regained his breath, he kicked and pushed his way up just enough for a quick look aboard. No one was at the stern, except for the two horses in the small pen just behind the cabin. The back rail of the pen was low, allowing room for the rudder sweep that hung in the water just beside him. He quietly lifted himself up and over the low gunwale and moved to the back of the pen, dropping to one knee as he searched for any sign of people. As he looked, a woman came to the rear of the cabin top, turned and started down the ladder. Kavanagh looked past her and saw the head of a man. He was holding a rifle before him but looking at the bank.

Suddenly rifle fire came from the bank, and the whistle of bullets overhead was heard. Those atop and within the cabin returned fire just as the woman at the ladder touched the deck. Kavanagh jumped up and grabbed her, stifling a scream with his meaty hand over her mouth and an arm around her waist. She kicked and tried to bite until he snarled into her ear, "Be still or I'll break your neck!"

Persis felt the strength of the man and knew he could easily break her neck or any other bone he chose. She quit kicking, grabbing at the man's arm and hand, fighting for air, but he pulled her against him and growled again, "Be still! If anyone hears you, I'll kill you and them!"

Having no idea what kind of weapons he had, she forced herself to go limp, searching for anything she could use against the brute.

Kavanagh grabbed a strip of leather from a packsaddle on the fence rail, pulled his wet handkerchief from his pocket, and stuffed it in her mouth, then, using the strip, he bound her hands in front of her and made a quick wrap around the rail with the end, securing her tight to the pole. Snatching up the halters, he put them on the two packhorses, and, turning to Persis, he asked, "Are there any saddles?" She looked wide-eyed and shook her head no, fearing what he planned.

He dropped the rail from the pen and moved the horses into position to leave the boat, then hissed into Persis' ear, "As soon as this boat touches the bank, we're goin' over the side with these horses. And don't you try anything or you're dead!" He lifted her atop the sorrel, wrapping the end of the leather strip that bound her hands into the mane of the horse to secure her atop the animal.

The rifle fire had subsided and the boat was moving to the shore, with Kavanagh pushing the sorrel with Persis aboard up against the back of the cabin to ensure she could not be seen by the man at the tiller, whose eyes were focused on the bank anyway. A long strip of sandbank backed by a grassy flat gave the flatboat an easy landing, and as soon as movement stopped, Kavanagh swung atop the chestnut, grabbed the lead of the sorrel, and leaning forward along the neck of his mount, then dug heels into its ribs, and forced the mount to the edge of the boat, and with a few more kicks and by slapping its rump with the tail end of the lead rope, the hesitant gelding gathered himself and made the leap to the sandbank. The sorrel balked, almost jerking Kavanagh off his mount, but the bull of a man yanked at the lead and the sorrel followed the chestnut onto the sandbank. Kavanagh gave a quick grin and clapped his legs to his mount, and the two horses went to the tall grass and soon disappeared into the thick brush.

* * * * *

Gabriel and Ezra pushed through the tangled brush, trying to get to the flatboat as quickly as possible. As they came to a large boulder that seemed out of place, Gabriel shinnied up on top to get a better view. He stretched to his full height to see over the thick spice brush and arrow wood. The boat was still over two hundred yards away and was putting into shore, but Gabriel was surprised to see someone atop the packhorses as they jumped to the shore and took off at a run into the grass flats and shrubbery beyond.

He scowled, then slipped off the boulder as Ezra asked, "What? What's wrong?"

"Somebody just took off with the packhorses! I think it mighta been Persis and maybe her brother, but . . ." he paused, shaking his head as he looked at his friend.

"Maybe something or somebody got left behind, and they're goin' after 'em," suggested Ezra, following close on Gabriel's heels.

"Yeah, maybe," replied Gabriel, stepping away from the boulder. He pointed to a break in the brush, "This way!"

As they pushed through the last of the tangles and brambles, Lucius spotted them and hollered, "Boy, am I glad to see you! One o' them pirates stole Persis and your packhorses!"

Gabriel looked to Ezra, and the two men stood frozen in thought until Gabriel affirmed, "I'll go get our horses! You make sure everything here's all right, then get some help to gather up the dead men's rifles and such. The boat'll need the extra firepower." He handed his Ferguson, the saddle pistol, and the bow and quiver to his friend, needing to climb the hill to retrieve the horses quickly. He spun on his heel and disappeared into the brush.

Ezra went to the boat, telling the captain about the position of the keelboat and the toll taken by him and Gabriel. "I'll take a man with me to gather up the other rifles and such. You ready yourselves for a possible attack from the keelboat. I don't think they will, but . . ."

"Take the boy, Boxley. Rufus was killed and Hamish was wounded, but we'll do what we can. You put a hurry on gettin' them other rifles. We can use 'em!"

"The confluence of the Ohio and Kanawha Rivers is on the east bank just above and across from Gallipolis. We'll wait at Gallipolis for two days, no more, for your return. There's a bit of a settlement at the confluence called Point Pleasant, but there's not much there. I'm certain you can find somebody with a boat that can come across to Gallipolis and give us word," explained the captain.

"I've put together a few things for you," interjected Charlotte, and she handed him a bundle wrapped in oilskin. "Tain't much, but it'll keep you goin'. Now, you get that girl back now, y'hear?"

"We'll do our best, ma'am," answered Gabriel as he swung aboard the big black. "And we thank you," he said, lifting the package. He spun the big stallion around and started off at a canter, following the clear trail made when the fleeing horses trampled the grass and brush. He had explained to Lucius about his sighting from the hilltop of the keelboat heading downstream and gave his opinion that with their numbers depleted, they would have to recruit more men before attempting another attack on anyone.

"So, you really think those pirates won't try again?" asked Ezra as the two men slowed their horses to a quick walk, giving them a breather.

"That bunch is like most freebooters, they'll only take on what they know they can overpower easily. Most bullies and thugs are really cowards, afraid of a real fight. When they've got their victims outnumbered, outgunned, and taken by surprise, they're assured of an easy victory. But once they have to face someone who is their equal, they'll turn tail and run," pronounced Gabriel.

"That sounds a bit philosophical," answered Ezra, looking at his friend with a touch of skepticism.

"Think about it, Ezra. How many times have we seen the bully types do exactly that? Just like this bunch before, when they were repulsed, they had to recruit more so they would once again have greater numbers. If they had tried to take our boat with the same numbers, seven men and two women, they'd be at the bottom of the river right now!"

"There!" Gabriel pointed, seeing the tracks leading into the bottom of the Ice Creek draw. Gabriel knew the packhorses were fresher than their saddle horses, he and Ezra having ridden them most of the morning in their pursuit of the keelboat. But they had rested for a couple of hours and grazed on the tall grass at the clearing atop the hill and were now anxious and eager on the trail. Plus, it was evident by the path taken by the pirate that he was neither a horseman nor a woodsman. Rather than holding to the obvious game trail, he chose his own route, often having to turn back when his path was blocked by thick timber and undergrowth.

"He's taken that draw!" declared Gabriel, looking at a sandy-bottomed narrow valley that turned back to the west. An obvious trail parted the trees and showed promise of easier going.

"At least he made a good choice here!" suggested Ezra as the two men took to the trail, Gabriel leaning far down for a better look at the tracks. He watched as his friend lifted his eyes to the cut between the hills, turned to look at him, and nodded.

Ezra recognized that old look of determination in Gabriel's eyes and knew he would not give up on this chase.

31 / Search

Kavanagh, always the brute and bully, had little or no respect for anyone or anything and used whatever was at hand for his own purposes, showing little regard for consequences. When he found himself in the water, his only goal was to escape, but knowledge of the nearness of their reward nagged at him, forcing him to try to make sense of the fight. He had seen Shorty, Hitch, and Burns take hits and knew that if they weren't dead, they probably would be soon, so he thought of the reward they sought for the head of Stonecroft as his and his alone. But how to get it without sharing it with anyone was the problem.

The lead rope burned his hand as the cantankerous sorrel that held the woman fought his rough handling. He growled as he yanked on the lead, jerking the horse's head around and making her stumble. The sorrel, usually a sure-footed animal, caught her balance and gained her footing to follow the beast on the chestnut. Persis struggled to keep her seat aboard the packhorse, her hands bound to the mane, using every bit of her experience aboard a horse. She fought for air, the wet handkerchief stuffed in her mouth hurting her jaws and making it difficult to breathe.

Kavanagh pulled up behind a finger ridge of thick trees to check his back trail. He knew they would come after him, and that was what he was counting on. Never the one for shrewd thinking, he knew that the men they pursued, the one known as Gabriel Stonecroft and his Negra friend, were suspected of being the two that had the horses aboard the flatboat. Although he had never met Stonecroft, they had a description of him and his friend, and so far, their best prospects were the two aboard the flatboat. That was why he took the woman, so she could tell him for sure if they were the ones they sought. At least, that was one of the reasons. He chuckled as he thought about being alone in the woods with this woman, then shook his head as he reminded himself that no woman was worth the five hundred dollars he could get for Stonecroft, and maybe another five hundred for his head in a bucket!

Seeing no one on his trail, he jerked the head of his horse around and, pulling at the lead rope of the other, started out again on the trail he followed. He had thought it would be necessary to try to catch up to the keelboat, but the more he thought about it, maybe not. After all, the man Shorty had said was their partner would want a share of the reward, and now that he considered the money as his alone, he saw no need to share. He would just have to come up with some other way of taking Stonecroft's head back to Philadelphia in a bucket.

Their horses were lathered up and their heads were hanging as he tried to force them back to a canter, but their stumbling almost unseated both riders and Kavanagh begrudgingly pointed them into the trees to a small clearing and dropped to the ground. He growled at Persis, "I'm gettin' you down, but don't try nuthin'. Won't bother me none at all to wring your scrawny neck!" Once the mane was disentangled from the bonds, he yanked her off the horse and dropped her on the ground. Grabbing the leather thong at her wrists, he dragged her to a tree, and let her straighten up to lean against the rough bark.

She looked at her captor with big, frightened eyes, mumbling around the cloth in her mouth, trying to plead with him to at least take out the gag. He grabbed at the cloth, roughly jerking it from her mouth and allowing her to take a deep breath, but she was almost sorry she had. The stench of his foul body and the sweat from the horses was overwhelming, and she coughed repeatedly.

"Cut that out!" he demanded, standing over her and scowling. "Now tell me, that man with the Negra, his name Stonecroft?"

Persis looked up at the man, terrified by his demeanor, and slowly nodded her head, wondering what this man wanted with Gabriel. Then she remembered Gabriel speaking of a bounty that might have been offered for his return, and she regretted answering her captor's question. When she saw the beast grinning at her response, she knew what he was after, but she was more afraid of what he might do to her. She drew her knees up to her chest and wrapped her arms around them, pulling herself into a tight ball and hoping she might die before succumbing to his demands.

* * * * *

The running horses left an easy-to-follow trail. The rich soil of the hills and valleys, deep with the loam of decayed and rotted timber and grasses, brought forth a bounty of greenery, while the sharp hooves of running horses dug deep and threw clods of black soil as they sought for footing on the slick grasses. Gabriel and Ezra kept a tireless pace with the horses eager to run, but time and distance were taking their toll on the already-well-used horses. The men held the animals to a ground-eating gait but often reined them back to a walk, letting them catch their breath and steady themselves.

"That man's using up those horses! They can't keep up this pace very long!" observed Gabriel as the two men walked theirs side by side.

"You're right about that! But I don't think he cares. I'm more concerned about the woman!" answered Ezra.

Gabriel snatched a sidelong glance at his friend, "Don't you think I am too?"

"Yeah, but . . ." then standing in his stirrups, Ezra pointed, "Looks like he went around that point. Better watch yourself!"

Rounding the point of trees and seeing the trail continue, both men leaned over to the side for a better look at the sign. "He musta been checkin' his backtrail," declared Gabriel, then reined the big black around to look in the direction of the tracks. They were in a saddle between two taller hills, and they could see the likely route of the trail they followed and what appeared to be a sizable meadow beyond, and possibly the river in the distance. He lifted his eyes to the sun, then back to the trail. "I been thinkin'. It looks like he's tryin' to make his way back around to the river, probably to catch up with his friends on the keelboat. He could be hidin' in any of these little draws or around any of these hills. Now, maybe if you went along the tree line on the west side there," pointing to the hillsides at the edge of the opening valley, "and I take the other side, we might make better time instead of following every zig and zag of his trail. That way, we could cut his sign if he tries to go back in the trees."

Shortly after the two split up, Gabriel cut the trail of the two packhorses turning up a draw and into the thicker timber. He stood in his stirrups and craned around, trying to see further into the trees, but failing that, he turned toward the opposite side of the widening valley and sounded out with the usual screaming cry of the red-tailed hawk, the friends' common call to one another. He waited, listening, then tried the descending scream again, but still no answer. Believing Ezra to be too far away or too deep in the woods to hear, he chose to follow the tracks alone, knowing Ezra would circle around until he too cut the trail and followed.

A narrow, meandering stream crowded with spicebush and dogwood chuckled from behind the thick brush, seeking its way to the lowlands. The prints of the horses showed they were now moving at a walk, but side by side. Gabriel repeatedly looked ahead, fearful of coming upon the kidnapper unexpectedly. He leaned low on the neck of the big black, searching for any anomaly to the tracks that would be a giveaway. He reined up and looked ahead, seeing the churned soil marking where the pursued pair had turned toward the trees.

Slowly and quietly, Gabriel stepped down, taking the reins to lead the big black into the trees at the edge of the narrow draw. Watching each step, staying in the deeper grass, he held one hand on the nose of the stallion, concerned about him smelling the sorrel mare and nickering. But although Ebony tossed his head, ears forward, and looked toward the deeper woods, he made not a sound. Gabriel whispered to his horse, "Good boy, good boy. Easy, now. I'm gonna tether you right here, but I'll be back soon." He stroked the black's head and neck, then, with rifle in hand, he turned into the trees, hearing the black already munching on the grass.

It took him almost a quarter-hour to move less than a hundred yards through the trees. Thick underbrush, downed timber, and no trail made a stealthy approach difficult, but he heard the movement of the horses and the low murmur of voices and worked his way carefully forward. He dropped to one knee and peered from behind the thick trunk of a towering black willow to see a big man crouched behind Persis, knife at her throat and an arm around her midriff.

He was looking directly at Gabriel when he growled, "You! In the trees! Show yersef now, or else I'll slit her throat!"

Gabriel slowly stood and walked from behind the tree,

rifle at his side. Kavanagh laughed, "Your own horses give you away! They was lookin' and watchin' as you come close. I knew somebody was comin'," he cackled a laugh again. "Now, come on out'chere an' lemme have a look at'chu!"

Gabriel slowly approached as the brute growled again, "Drop yer rifle right there!" he ordered, pulling the knife closer to Persis' throat. Her eyes were wide and filled with tears. Gabriel could see that her hands were bound, and a rag had been tied over her mouth; but every time she tried to move, Kavanagh pulled her tight against him.

"Now that pistol, drop it!"

Gabriel slowly slipped the pistol from his belt, holding lightly to the butt, and bent his knees to drop the weapon into the grass beside the rifle. Kavanagh laughed, "Ain't so high an' mighty now are ya, *Mister Stonecroft?*" He snarled and let the corner of his upper lip curl up as he flared his nostrils. "And you ain't gonna look so good after I put yore head in a bucket an' take it back to that ol' man in Philadelphia neither!"

"Look, if it's me you want, why don't you let her go? I'll go with you, and you can leave her be," suggested Gabriel, holding one hand out to indicate his sincerity.

"Ha! I got the both of you, and I'm gonna do whatever I please, and ain't nuthin' you can do about it! Now, move away from them guns!" he demanded, waving the knife toward him.

Gabriel sidestepped away from his weapons and added, "Look, she's just gonna get in your way and be more trouble. Let her go, let her have a horse, and we can catch up to your friends in a couple hours. She won't even find her way out of the woods by that time."

"Uh-uh. I'm keepin' her! But first, I'm gonna kill you so you won't be any trouble! An' she's gonna watch while I cut your head right off'n your neck!" he snarled, pushing Persis aside, causing her to stumble and fall. He kicked at her, "Stay outta the way an' don't try nuthin', 'cuz I can kill you just as easy!"

Kavanagh dropped into a crouch, holding his knife hand wide to the side and the other arm outstretched as he began moving toward Gabriel. When Kavanagh was far enough away from Persis, Gabriel told her, "Stay back, Persis, I'll take care of this blowhard!"

Kavanagh rose up and growled, starting his charge toward Gabriel, but stopped suddenly when Gabriel's knife appeared in his hand and a wide grin crossed his face. This man was supposed to be in fear of his life, but he had dropped into a crouch, knife held lightly, blade up and started circling the big brute, Kavanagh. An experienced knife-fighter, Kavanagh laughed. "What'chu think you can do with that toad-sticker? I'm gonna gut you with your own knife, boy!"

"That all you can do, is talk about it?" asked Gabriel, slowly moving his knife side to side.

Kavanagh was reading the movements of the younger and smaller man, and these were the moves of an experienced fighter, but he wasn't concerned. He had killed men on the rolling decks of ships, in the dark alleys of the city, and aboard flatboats and keelboats, and he knew he could handle this whippersnapper. He feinted with his knife and tried a round-house swing with his left, but Gabriel ducked under the swing and made a deft move to slice at the side of the bigger man, drawing blood. Kavanagh growled, eyes flaring as he spun back toward Gabriel, but he was out of reach. The pirate made a sudden sweep with his knife at Gabriel's middle, but the young man sucked in his gut and went up on tiptoe and the blade only notched his buckskin tunic. Gabriel parried and cut the forearm of Kavanagh.

Facing one another again, Kavanagh tried the fool's trick of tossing his knife from hand to hand, trying to frighten Gabriel with his cunning and knife-handling, but Gabriel watched and, quicker than a snake's strike, he knocked Kavanagh's knife away, then slapped the man's face and backhanded it just as quick. Anger flared in Kavanagh's eyes and he tried a bull charge, making Gabriel backpedal but the big man caught him, wrapping his arms around him and pinning Gabriel's arms to his side. Kavanagh growled and lifted Gabriel off the ground, squeezing him with all his strength, forcing Gabriel's breath from his lungs and making him gasp for air. His feet off the ground, he tried kicking but connected with nothing, then, mustering the last of his strength, he arched his back and brought his forehead forward like a sledge on a stake and smashed Kavanagh's nose, splattering blood across his face and loosening his grip just enough to allow Gabriel to squirm free.

He dropped to the ground, sucking for air and trying to crawl out of reach, but a meaty paw grabbed his ankle and pulled. Gabriel spun around, twisting his leg and kicking with his free foot that found the broken nose of Kavanagh and brought a scream from the man. Gabriel jumped to his feet, realized he still had his knife gripped tightly in his hand, and faced the bloody beast before him.

The macabre monster stared from his bloody face, snarling and growling like the beast he was, and charged the object of his wrath. Gabriel dropped into a crouch, and as the big man came on, screaming and growling, Gabriel stepped to the side and plunged the knife to its hilt in the man's gut. He never slowed his charge. His outstretched arms grabbed at Gabriel again and caught hold of his tunic, but Gabriel had extracted the knife and lowered his shoulder to bring the blade up and into the man's side, driving it in to its hilt. As they scrambled, he pulled it out and drove it in again and again, but Kavanagh never slowed. He lunged at Gabriel, and as the younger man backpedaled, his foot dropped into a hole and Kavanagh slammed him to his back, all of the man's weight falling atop him and driving the air from his lungs.

Gabriel fought for air and Kavanagh lifted up off his torso but stayed astraddle of the younger man. Gabriel was shocked to see that Kavanagh had found his knife and now held it high above his head, making Gabriel wonder how this man could still be alive. "Now I'm gonna cut that purty little head off!" He pushed down on Gabriel's shoulder with all the force and weight of his free hand and raised the knife hand high. Kavanagh's knees were on Gabriel's hands, and the sheer weight of the man as he sat astraddle of Gabriel kept the younger man helpless. His eyes were wide, and as he watched the blade, he saw Kavanagh suck in wind and snarl with his lip curled, face dripping blood on Gabriel's chest and death showing in his eyes. Gabriel glared as the knife slowly started its descent and came ever nearer, until a sudden blast preceded the explosion of Kavanagh's head, knocking the man from Gabriel's chest and allowing the younger man to breathe again.

He lifted his head to look at the still form of the beast and scrambled to his feet before the big man could move again, then, looking around, saw a grinning Ezra standing at the edge of the clearing with a smoking long rifle in his hand. He shook his head, "You just can't help it, can you? Get outta my sight for a few minutes, and you land smack in the middle of trouble! What am I gonna do with you?"

32 / Point Pleasant

"We won't make it back to the boat in time, will we?" asked Persis. She was sitting on Gabriel's bedroll behind the cantle of his saddle, both arms around his middle and her cheek resting on his back.

"No, but we'll make a comfortable camp yonder," he answered, pointing with his chin toward a notch in a flat-top bluff. Ten-mile Creek meandered through the brush about twenty feet from the timber that held to the south face, and it would provide ample water for both the horses and the riders. He nodded to Ezra and watched as his friend gigged his horse toward the notch, making sure they wouldn't be encroaching on anyone's camp. The last thing they wanted was an unfriendly confrontation with some Shawnee.

Persis took the bundle given to the men by Charlotte and went to the fire. Gabriel was tending to the horses, giving each a good rubdown with the turkeyfoot grass while Ezra tended the fire, gathering more wood and arranging some rocks around the embers to keep the fire contained. He fetched the coffee pot and some coffee beans and set about grinding the beans on the rocks while Charlotte sought to make the best of their limited rations. Charlotte's bundle held several biscuits and slices of meat that Persis added to the pot of wild onions, mushrooms, and sunflower roots.

After finishing their meal, they were sitting back, enjoying the last of the coffee and each having a handful of raspberries and strawberries, Gabriel asked Persis, "Have you thought much about what you're going to do? I mean, now that Rufus is gone?"

Persis dropped her eyes to the fire, slowly shaking her head. "I just can't believe he's gone. I mean, I know he is, but we have never been apart for more than a day, and he's like the other half of me!" A sob choked her, and she dabbed at the tears that threatened to overflow.

"My sister and I were close, not like you and Rufus, you two bein' twins and all, but the thought of losing her? Well, I guess what I'm saying is, I hurt for you," said Gabriel, stirring the embers with a long willow stick.

"Charlotte asked me to stay with her at Gallipolis, but that was before. Now, maybe that would be my best way. It was Rufus' plan to go back to England, although we've never been there, and I just have no idea what to do if I did go there. But Charlotte said she has a home, and maybe we could do some dressmaking or . . ." Her thoughts trailed off with her voice, and a glaze crossed her eyes as she stared at the glowing embers.

Ezra looked to his friend, "What about you? What are you gonna do?"

Gabriel frowned, "Me? What do you mean?" showing his confusion with a wrinkled brow.

"I mean, that was about as close as you've ever come to crossing the great divide, and you're not ready. So?"

Persis turned and looked at Gabriel, "You mean you're not ready for eternity? Don't you believe in the hereafter?"

"So, now the two of you are gangin' up on me, are you?"

Ezra didn't answer but stood and went to his saddlebags and retrieved his Bible and then to Gabriel's for his. When he returned to the fire, he tossed Gabriel's Bible to his friend and sat down across from him. He looked to Persis, who sat nearer to Gabriel, "You show him where these verses are when I get to 'em, all right?" She smiled, nodding as she scooted to Gabriel's side, then looked to Ezra as a sign for him to begin.

Ezra leaned forward, "Look, my friend, we've talked about this before and you said you were concerned and interested, but after today, it's more than just being interested. Because of my father being a preacher, I learned these things long ago, and I've always been at peace about where I stand with the Lord and where I would spend eternity. This," he motioned to all that was around them with a swing of his hand, "is all temporary. What really counts is eternity, and the Bible tells us we can know where we'll spend that eternity and tells us how. That's what I want to show you. Now, turn to Romans chapter three, verse ten. There's four things you need to understand."

In the waning hours of the evening, the three friends perused the Scriptures as Ezra showed his friend the four things he needed to know. That everyone is a sinner, (Romans 3:10, 23), the penalty for that sin is eternal death, (Romans 5:12, 6:23) but Christ paid that penalty for us so we wouldn't have to, (Romans 5:8) and the free gift He offers because He paid that penalty is eternal life (Romans 6:23). "Now, the most important thing to know is, because Jesus paid that penalty and offers us a free gift of eternal life, it's just like any other gift; you have to accept it. Now, here in Romans chapter ten, verses nine through thirteen, he tells us all we have to do is pray, believing in our heart in what He has done. Ask for that gift, and it's ours!"

"Just like that?" asked Gabriel. "I thought I'd have to go to church and do something else. You know, get baptized or join the church or sing in the choir or somethin'."

Ezra chuckled and dropped his head as he shook it in consternation, then lifted his eyes to his friend, "Gabriel, there's nothing any of us can do that would cause us to deserve Heaven. It's all because of what He's done for us. If it was up to us, we'd come up with all kinds of good deeds and run around braggin' about them all the time. Now, I know there's folks who think like that, but Ephesians 2:8-9 says it's by God's grace we are saved, not by the good works we do, because like I said, we'd all go around bragging about it."

"So, if I do like you said, pray and ask for that gift of eternal life, it's mine?"

"Yes, but you must believe it with all your heart. That's why it's called a gift. If we had to earn it, it wouldn't be a gift," added Ezra, looking to his friend and Persis.

"So, would you help me? Pray, I mean. I'm not too good at it," asked Gabriel.

The three friends bowed their heads, and Ezra led them in prayer. When he told Gabriel he should pray in his own words and ask God to forgive him for his sins and to give him that free gift of eternal life, Gabriel, in his university-correct English, asked humbly for that gift. When he finished, the three friends said a collective "Amen," and looked to one another, content with what had been said and done.

Dawn kicked the three from their blankets to the accompaniment of an enthusiastic red-bellied woodpecker hammering his way into a still-standing dead poplar. The rhythmic rat-a-tat hastened the three on their journey to be reunited with the flatboat crew. Just before the sun was at its zenith, they rode from the trees onto the rich bottomland, where crops of corn and wheat waved in the wind. Two cabins were nestled near the trees and on the banks of the Kanawha River at its confluence with the Ohio. Gabriel looked at Ezra, "This must be what Lucius called Point Pleasant, and if I remember my history correctly, some have said this was where the first battle of the Revolutionary War was fought. It's where Colonel Lewis fought a confederation of Shawnee and Mingo led by ol' Chief Cornstalk. Big battle it was, too. Some records say there were over a thousand on each side, but Colonel Lewis and his men did quite a fine job."

"Wasn't there a fort here at one time?" asked Ezra, looking around.

"Fort Randolph, I think it was, but I believe it's long abandoned. Don't see any sign of a fort, do you?" asked Gabriel.

They saw a couple standing in front of one of the cabins as they neared, and with a friendly wave, the three approached the settlers. "How do, folks!" started Gabriel, leaning forward on the pommel of his saddle. "We're looking for someone to get our horses and us across the Ohio, we're headin' to Gallipolis to meet up with our friends. Would there be someone about who could get us across?"

The couple stood before them, shading their eyes as they looked up at the three, and the man stepped closer, "Just the four horses an' you?" he asked.

Gabriel grinned, "Yessir, just what you see here."

The woman who stood behind her man said, "Well, ask 'em, Jed."

The man lifted his hand, "I'm Jedediah Holcomb, and this is my wife, Justis. She wants you folks to sit to a meal with us, if'n you'd like."

The three smiled at the invitation, and Persis answered for them, "We'd love to join you." She slid to the ground, with a hand from Gabriel, "I'm sorry we don't have anything to add to the meal, but we would enjoy sitting with you folks." The women joined hands and disappeared into the cabin without a backward glance at the men. Jedidiah looked at Gabriel, "You can water your horses there," he nodded toward the water trough, "and put 'em in the corral with Betsy an' Mable, muh mules. They gets along with anything, so t'won't be no trouble. If you'd like to wash up, there's a basin beside the house."

"Thank you," said Gabriel as he stepped down. "But, do you know anyone who can help us across the river?"

"Yup, I got a bit of a barge yonder. It'll get you'n yours across, alright. But I'll need to take muh mules downstream a ways first. We can pole acrost, then I can get it back, but I need muh mules to pull it back upstream." He had stood watching as they tended to their horses. He was barefooted, with high-water britches held up with galluses that stretched over a tattered linen shirt. "Thought about riggin' up a ferry sorta thing, but don't get 'nuff folks comin' through to make it pay."

Gabriel offered, "We'll be happy to pay for your trouble. It would be worth it to us." He grabbed the soiled flour sack that served as a towel, wiped his hands, and thought for a minute, "Let's see, the last ferry we used charged fifty cents per horse and fifteen cents per man. So, you think two dollars and fifty cents would cover it?"

The settler's eyes grew wide, "Shore would! That'd be mighty fine, yessir! We'ns don't get much in the way of real money here'bouts, an' that'd suit me just fine."

Gabriel dug into his britches pocket and brought out some coins, picked out two silver dollars and one fifty-cent piece, and handed them to Jedidiah. The settler accepted the coins, then looked at each one and turned them over, "They sure is shiny!"

Gabriel chuckled, "We came from Philadelphia, and those were minted just this year. Get a little wear and tear on 'em and they won't be so shiny."

Jedidiah mumbled, "Ma gets her way, they won't see the light of day again!"

33 / Gallipolis

While Persis stood before the horses, occasionally stroking their heads and necks and talking to them, the men poled and paddled the flatboat across the current of the Ohio. In the depths of the current, they were busy with the long oars that resembled the sweeps of the big flatboat they were used to, and they handled them well as Jedidiah manned the rudder. The morning crossing was over placid water and the lazy current pushed them downstream, but they made the far bank without incident. When the boat nosed into the sandbank, Ezra jumped off to secure the line to give them time to offload the horses. Once ashore, they helped push off the boat and mounted quickly as they watched Jedidiah navigate the current to cross back to the Virginia territory side.

The river crossing was easier than expected, and Jedidiah was more than happy with the new coins in his pocket. Mid-afternoon saw the trio arriving at the gates of the palisades that led to the town square of the French settlement, Gallipolis.

Unique in its order, several cabins lined the outside walls of the palisade, which also had three bastions at the prominent corners. Behind the fort-like structure sat four rows of almost identical and closely aligned log cabins, each accommodating a family or an individual tradesman. The community was made up of those referred to as "the French 500" and was led by Count Jean-Joseph de Barth, a former member of the French National Assembly.

The word quickly passed among the community, and before the trio set foot on the ground, they heard the squeal of delight that came from Charlotte as she ran to the side of the big black and stretched her hands up to help Persis down. "Oh, I am so relieved! I have never prayed so hard, and I was so worried for you!" declared Charlotte as she hugged Persis like a long-lost sister. She pushed her back to arm's length, "And look at you! Not a scratch on you! Why, you look like you just went out for a casual stroll, not a fight with a mad pirate!" She pulled her close and hugged her again. "Now, come with me. I have something to show you!" Hand in hand, the two women left the palisade. Gabriel and Ezra stood with their mouths open and stared as the two disappeared.

After a quick look around, Gabriel and Ezra led their horses down to the riverbank where they were told the flatboat was moored. Lucius saw them coming and stood atop the cabin, waving a welcome. As they neared, he frowned and leaned down, "Didn't you get the woman?"

Gabriel grinned, "Oh, yeah, we got her, and as soon as we entered the fort up there, Charlotte took her away faster'n the pirate did!"

Lucius, obviously relieved, smiled and stood, "That's good news! I'm glad for her! Much trouble?"

"Nothin' more'n we expected," answered Ezra, grinning.

"So, when are you pullin' out?" asked Gabriel, standing with reins in hand and Ebony pushing at his back, wanting to get to some grass nearby.

"First thing in the mornin', now that you're back!" He looked at the two, then added, "That is, if you're still coming with us. You are, aren't you?"

"We've been thinkin' on it. But for right now, we're gonna picket the horses on the grass yonder, take stock of what we've got and such, maybe get a touch of sleep, and then we'll talk about it. That all right with you, Captain?"

"Of course. We put the word out that we're here for some tradin' and we'll be busy the rest of the afternoon and part of the evening, so take your time, boys. You've earned it."

Once the horses were picketed and had settled into their grazing, Ezra suggested, "How 'bout we go find those women and see what they're up to?"

Gabriel chuckled, "That's exactly what I was thinking." The two friends laughed at one another as they started back to the palisade to find the women. Within the public square in what the men had initially thought were barracks or houses for some of the residents were quartered the many tradesmen and merchants who had set up their shops for the community. As they walked along the boardwalk in front of the hewn-log structures, small signs in the windows identified the different businesses. All of the signs were in French, and as near as Gabriel could make out, there was a surgeon, a watchmaker, a glassblower, a lawyer, a justice of the peace, a hatmaker, a tailor, and others, but most were tradesmen and craftsmen that were seldom found in other communities. Usually, a typical settlement in the frontier would have a trader, a livery, a tavern, and maybe a rooming house, but seldom the craftsmen found in Gallipolis.

As the men walked and explored, a voice came from behind them, "I see you have found us!"

They turned to see Charlotte and Persis, arms full of material and bundles, and the men quickly stepped in to give aid. Once the women were unburdened, Charlotte said, "Follow us. We have something to show you." She led them to one of the shops that stood empty, and they pushed open the door and entered. Charlotte stopped, hands out to her sides. "Isn't it wonderful?"

Gabriel, looking around the bundles he held, said, "Uh, if you say so, but what are we looking at?"

"Oh, I'm sorry. This is our new dress shop!" she declared, "Here, put the bundles on the table." She pointed to a long plank table that sat against the wall. The men set down the packages and the material, then turned to look around. The door stood open, and the one window, though somewhat dirty with fly-specks and accumulated dust and dirt, allowed the afternoon sun to send its lances of light into the sparse room. Charlotte began describing what they would do, the counters, tables, and benches to be built, and what they expected to accomplish as

Persis, smiling patiently, watched and listened.

"So, it sounds like you've got it planned out all right, and there are enough women here who will pay for dresses?" Gabriel asked, watching Persis as Charlotte spoke.

"There are over two hundred women, and many children, as well. And I don't know if you noticed, but very few of these women are used to daily labor. They, for the most part, come from families that are tradesmen and craftsmen, or men of the military, or nobility, or even professional men. That has been one of the difficulties; few know much of anything about farming, hunting, and other things necessary to survive in the wilderness. These are city folk, and as such, expect the comforts of the city," explained Charlotte.

Gabriel stepped closer to Persis, "Do you think you can be happy here?"

She dropped her eyes and spoke softly, "I have little choice. I have nothing to go back to, and no family. Charlotte has been very kind to include me in her plans, and yes, I think I can find happiness here." She lifted her eyes to Gabriel and they locked their gazes for several moments, until Gabriel turned away. His thoughts were circling, and he could wrestle with them no more. Try as he might, he could come to no other solution. If things were different, he might take her back to Philadelphia, but right now, he had no way of taking her anywhere. Here she would be safe and useful, and perhaps build a new life for herself. He was attracted to her and enjoyed her company, but such was not to be. He turned to the door.

"Well, we're gonna miss you! Both of you! Now we'll have

to put up with Ezra's cooking, and I'm not too sure if we're up to that!" declared Gabriel, standing in the door. Persis walked to him, slipped her arms around his waist, and lay her head on his chest. "You will always be precious to me, and I'll never forget you!" She leaned back to look up at this man who had saved her life and rescued her from the beast from the boat, "I wish you could stay too!"

Gabriel chuckled as he held her, "If things were different, I would. But you've already seen what can happen when those who are after a bounty come after me. I wouldn't bring any more danger upon you or this village for anything. No, it's best we keep to our plan and disappear in the unexplored West. There's much to find and do there, and maybe, just maybe, some time we might come back this way. You never know."

"Oh, please do! No matter when, you must try to come back. Promise me?" she pleaded.

"I promise that if circumstances allow, I will come back. But you have to promise me something too."

"Name it!" she answered, still holding him close and looking up at him with a broad smile.

"Don't live your life expecting me to return. Whatever comes your way, do as your heart leads. Where we are going, we are not promised even one tomorrow, and you cannot sacrifice your future on the slim possibility of what might never happen."

"I understand. And you do the same, alright?" she asked.

He smiled, hugged her tight, and stepped through the door to walk away, with Ezra at his side. They turned once to see the women standing in the doorway and waved, then quickened their pace to the boat.

The trading was good, and the cabin was getting crowded with pelts and other goods, mostly handcrafted items such as small furniture pieces, rifle stocks, and raw lumber. All the livestock had been traded off, leaving several barrels of whiskey, a few bags of staples, and the confiscated rifles and gear from the pirates. With the horses aboard, the first hint of grey morning light saw the boat catching the current and resuming its journey on the Ohio. Gabriel stood atop the cabin and watched the rising sun cast its drops of rose and orange onto the ripples of the river. Lucius negotiated the wide bend, and the river lined out southward. Gabriel looked downstream at the tree-lined banks and the lazy waters before them, letting his mind wander to the days ahead.

It would be another six or seven weeks before they made the Mississippi, and the trees that now stood bedecked in their summer coats of green would doff the drab colors in favor of the multi-hued splendor of fall. The cold weather would be threatening, and if they were lucky, they would be ashore on the west bank of the Mississippi, and their horses would be pointed west. He smiled at the thought of the discoveries that lay before them and whatever adventures might come, but he also thought with a touch of melancholy about the home and family he had left behind.

But he firmly believed he had a destiny of discovery before him, waiting for his arrival.

A LOOK AT: DISCOVERY OF DESTINY (STONECROFT SAGA 2)

AUTHOR OF THE BEST-SELLING BUCKSKIN CHRON-ICLES SERIES TAKES US ON AN EPIC JOURNEY IN BOOK TWO OF THE STONECROFT SAGA

Two friends committed to one another and their destiny of exploring the wilderness known as French Louisiana. A land that would soon become the Louisiana Purchase and a part of the growing nation of the United Colonies. But another man, wealthy, influential and vindictive is determined to see Gabriel Stonecroft pay the ultimate price for the death of his son, a ne'er do well troublemaker who surrendered his life in a duel with Stonecroft. After a perilous journey down the Ohio River aboard a flatboat, the two friends now set out to explore the west. But local toughs in the young town of New Madrid pick a fight and earn nothing but wounds and a grudge, a grudge that will be nursed by bounty hunters that seek to collect the sizable reward offered for the head of this young, would-be explorer. But when they find a runaway captive of the Pawnee, and fight alongside the Osage Warriors, the most feared fighters in the new land, the plans of the two friends take a drastic detour. Land-locked pirates team up with bounty hunters and renegade Indians to do their best to permanently change the plans of the two adventuresome friends. And when women enter the picture, everything changes.

AVAILABLE FEBRUARY 2020

ABOUT THE AUTHOR

Born and raised in Colorado into a family of ranchers and cowboys, B.N. Rundell is the youngest of seven sons. Juggling bull riding, skiing, and high school, graduation was a launching pad for a hitch in the Army Paratroopers. After the army, he finished his college education in Springfield, MO, and together with his wife and growing family, entered the ministry as a Baptist preacher.

Together, B.N. and Dawn raised four girls that are now married and have made them proud grandparents. With many years as a successful pastor and educator, he retired from the ministry and followed in the footsteps of his entrepreneurial father and started a successful insurance agency, which is now in the hands of his trusted nephew. He has also been a successful audiobook narrator and has recorded many books for several award-winning authors. Now finally realizing his life-long dream, B.N. has turned his efforts to writing a variety of books, from children's picture books and young adult adventure books, to the historical fiction and western genres.